A JOHN BEKKER MYSTERY

SUNSET

AL LAMANDA

KENNEBEC LARGE PRINT
A part of Gale, Cengage Learning

GALE
CENGAGE Learning®

Detroit • New York • San Francisco • New Haven, Conn • Waterville, Maine • London

GALE
CENGAGE Learning

LIBRARY OF CONGRESS CATALOGING-IN-PUBLICATION DATA

Lamanda, Al.
  Sunset / by Al Lamanda.
    pages ; cm. — (Kennebec Large Print superior collection) (A John Bekker mystery)
    ISBN 978-1-4104-5566-6 (softcover) — ISBN 1-4104-5566-1 (softcover) 1. Ex-police officers—Fiction. 2. Alcoholics—Fiction. 3. Wives—Crimes against—Fiction. 4. Large type books. I. Title.
PS3612.A5433S86 2013
813'.6—dc23   2012041099

Published in 2013 by arrangement with Tekno Books and Ed Gorman

Printed in the United States of America
1 2 3 4 5   17 16 15 14 13

For Maryann, a
very courageous woman

1

Carol laughed more than any person I've ever met. At jokes, comedies, at our daughter when she did something funny the way little girls do. She loved sunsets, snowstorms, and chocolate. If she could no longer fit into her favorite jeans, she'd cut out the broccoli instead of the chocolate. She cried at every dog movie, even if the dog lived at the end. We went to Yellowstone Park once before our daughter was born. A black bear the size of a Volkswagen invaded our cooler. I watched as Carol picked up a stick and chased the bear away. She actually used the word *shoo.* A year after our daughter was born, she called me on a stakeout, terrified because a mouse was in the house. She wouldn't get off the kitchen table until I came home. She went to church on a regular basis, but could swear like a sailor on leave when provoked. She loved Christmas trees and would keep one up year round if she could.

Carol lived thirty-three years.

We were married for eleven of those years.

It wasn't nearly long enough.

There's a hole in my heart where my life used to be.

A man invaded our home one morning after I'd left for work. He was sent to deliver a message. I was to back off the murder investigation I was involved in or else. The man caught Carol in the shower. He got carried away. He raped and strangled her in front of our five-year-old daughter.

My daughter, her name is Regan, hasn't spoken a word in twelve years. She resides in a medical facility in the country where they care for her every need. She plays with crayons and watches Bugs Bunny a lot. Regan will never go to her prom, wear a graduation gown, or have a first kiss.

I used to visit Regan every week.

I don't anymore.

I drink instead.

2

My day began the way it has for the past decade or so. I didn't so much wake up as come to. The night before, I didn't go to sleep, but pass out. When my eyes opened, there were sixty seconds or so of blurred dizziness before I stumbled to the bathroom and vomited up the remains of a fifth of scotch.

It burned as much coming out as going down. The taste and odor were foul.

When my stomach settled, I washed my face with cold water until my eyes functioned. Then I grabbed a beer from the fridge, stumbled outside, and sat in a lawn chair that faced the ocean.

The tide was rolling in. Waves crashed on the beach. Gulls patrolled for bits of leftovers and anything else edible they could find.

I sipped beer and waited for results.

The sun was warm. I glanced at it and

judged the time somewhere between eleven and eleven-thirty. I wasn't in the Navy. I couldn't tell time by the sun, the stars, or navigate at night. I just knew where the sun should be at certain times of the day. I learned from sitting in a lawn chair and looking at it for a decade.

After Carol died and Regan was in the home, I would sit in our big empty house and cry myself to sleep on the sofa. The department shrink told me that wasn't healthy. He recommended I sell the house and move to a neighborhood where not everything would remind me of Carol and what I'd lost.

How do you explain to a shrink that what you lost is inside you, that you carry it around like the blood in your veins?

On the card table to my left was a pack of cigarettes, matches, and an overflowing ashtray. I lit a cigarette, sipped beer from the bottle, and listened to the waves crashing on the beach.

The beer was doing its job, settling things down to a nice even keel.

My vision cleared. The headache lessened.

A hundred yards to my right was my only neighbor on the otherwise deserted stretch of beach. I saw him walking toward me, cigarette between lips, beer in hand. His name was Ozzie, but I called him Oz. He was black, with snow-white hair, a scraggly speckled beard and was somewhere between sixty-eight and seventy years old. I didn't know for sure and never asked. He was here when I moved in ten years ago.

I smoked the cigarette while Oz walked toward the vacant chair on my right. He brought it over years ago and there it stayed, rain or shine. I guess he had no reason to bring it back.

"Gonna eat today?" Oz said when he arrived and took his chair.

"Thinking about it," I said.

Oz looked at the rusty grill in front of the card table. "Coals is still good," he said. "We could grill up some burgers?"

I lit another cigarette.

So did Oz.

We both sipped our beer.

"Your check arrive?" I said.

"This morning."

"Then so did mine," I said.

We sipped and smoked.

"You want to go to town or get the coals ready?" I said.

"Already been to town," Oz said. "To get my check."

"I'll go," I said.

Neither of us moved until the beers were

empty. I stood up. "I'll change clothes and go now," I said.

Ten minutes later, I came out of my trailer wearing cleaner, but not clean, jeans with a button-down corduroy shirt worn outside. I found the sunglasses I lost a week ago and slipped them on to cover my bloodshot eyes.

"Back in a bit," I said, walking away.

"John?" Oz called after me.

I turned around. "Yeah?"

"Don't get no rolls with them little seeds," Oz said. "They hurt my gut something awful."

"Right."

"And maybe get some baked beans," Oz said. "You know how much I like baked beans."

"Right."

Three quarters of a mile from my trailer was the center of town, the town of Bayridge. The town wasn't much, but neither was the bay. Kind of gray and gloomy, with a few shops and stores, a gas station, bank, and post office. If you called 911, it generally meant a one-hour wait for an ambulance or county sheriff. That kind of town.

I hit the post office first for my disability check. Sixteen years of police work earned me a forty percent pay disability with benefits pension. It wasn't much, but I didn't need much. All I ever bought was booze and occasionally some food.

I went from post office to bank to grocery. I bought burgers, a Tupperware of baked beans, some lemon squares, a six-pack of beer, and a fifth of scotch. I carried two large sacks back to my trailer where Oz was working the coals.

"Coals ready," Oz announced when I set the two sacks in my arms on the card table.

"Let's have a beer first," I said.

We had a beer.

Ours was a no-hurry world.

We had nothing to hurry for.

While the burgers sizzled over the coals and the baked beans heated in a saucepan on the grill, we sipped a second beer and watched the sun crawl across the sky.

"A game on tonight," Oz said.

"Who?"

"Yankees at Baltimore," Oz said. "It's a network game. They show what they show."

"I'll bring out the TV," I said.

We ate our burgers with baked beans and drank more beer until the beer was gone and we cracked the seal on the scotch. We ate the lemon squares while sipping scotch over ice in plastic cups as the coals cooled down along with the afternoon.

We weren't drunk, not by a long shot. We were maintenance drinking to keep our heads clear for the game. The drunk would come later. After the sun had gone down and we were alone in the dark to face our demons.

And ourselves.

"What I like with beans is cornbread," Oz said as he sipped scotch from his plastic cup. "I should have mentioned it before."

"I would have picked it up," I said.

"I know," Oz said. "My mistake. I'll remember next time."

We drank more scotch and smoked a few cigarettes.

"Them waves is acting up," Oz said.

I listened. The waves crashed against the beach and the rocks at the point. They produced a boom as they struck and a crackle when they receded. It was a pleasant enough sound to listen to while drinking scotch from a plastic cup.

My cup was empty. So was Oz's. I added ice from the bucket to each cup and splashed in some scotch, topping each off with some water. Later on, we would forgo the water, then the ice.

For now, our buzz was minor and we felt no pain.

Years ago, I asked Oz how he wound up

living in a trailer on the beach. His bleary, red eyes watered up and he said, "Don't never ask me that. Don't never ask me that again."

I didn't.

I found out by accident when I stumbled upon an old newspaper clipping in Oz's trailer several years ago when, after a hard night of drinking, I helped him to bed. The old clipping was taped to a bedside lamp. It was frayed and yellow, but still readable.

Twenty years ago, Oz was an average postal employee waiting for his pension. Home, grown kids, wife, the works. Driving home from a family gathering one afternoon, his youngest daughter in the backseat, a dump truck blindsided Oz's van, rolling it several times before it came to a stop in a ditch.

Oz's wife died on impact.

A flattened piece of scrap metal flew off the truck, crashed through the back window of Oz's van and decapitated his daughter. Her head wound up on his lap.

A reason to crawl inside a bottle?

I never brought it up and Oz has no idea I know.

We'll keep it that way.

"Game on soon," Oz said.

"I'll get the TV in a bit," I said.

We lit fresh cigarettes.

"You old enough to remember the M and M boys?" Oz said. "The wars between the Yankees and Brooklyn Dodgers?"

"I was a boy, but I remember," I said.

"Mays, Mantle, or Snider?"

"No doubt Snider was a good player, but he lacked the staying power," I said. "Mays was the greatest of them all, but Mantle was the most dramatic in the clutch. He had a way of getting it done when it counted and he did it with one good leg. People got excited watching him strike out."

"We'll never see that likes again," Oz commented.

"No, we won't. All three."

I got the TV. It was a nineteen-inch portable with rabbit ears that I set on the card table and ran with an extension cord. Without cable, all it picked up were the four networks and some local channels.

Neither of us cared.

Nothing on network interested us much except for the occasional movie or sporting event. Reality shows were comedies without being funny.

By the end of the third inning, the Yankees were up four to nothing over Baltimore. The Yankees were a great team. Baltimore was not.

We drank some more scotch, making a dent in the bottle.

"I got some microwave popcorn," I suggested.

"Buttered?"

"Believe so."

By the fifth inning, the Yankees led nine to one and we ate popcorn and drank scotch and really didn't care who won or lost, just that the game itself was a diversion.

At the seventh inning stretch, the bottle was low, the popcorn bowl empty, and we lost track of the score.

Oz fell asleep with one ounce of scotch left in the bottle. I poured that last ounce into my plastic cup and toasted the ballgame for lack of anything else to toast. My vision or lack of it was blurred to the point I could no longer see the score. My tongue was thick and heavy in my mouth. My senses were dull and reflexes gone.

I felt no pain.

That was where I wanted to live. The United States of no pain.

I steadied my hand enough to light a cigarette and sipped the last ounce of scotch.

Somehow, I wound up in bed and when I fell asleep or passed out, I was at peace.

When I opened my eyes next, I was greeted with a large gloved fist.

3

The upside of passing out drunk is that you don't dream. The downside is more often than not, when you come to you're soaked in your own piss and vomit at the sight of the toilet.

I knew I was coming toward the surface when I heard faint voices in the background of my brain. My dulled senses thought it was the TV left on all night. I began to see light through my closed eyelids.

A gruff voice said, "I think he's waking up."

Another voice said, "Don't let him. Give him the dope soon as he opens his eyes."

Through the fog and haze, my brain wondered what program that was on the TV.

My eyes opened. There was a moment of blurred fuzz. My vision cleared and I saw the gloved hand coming closer to my face. I saw the rag and smelled the ether. I lacked the strength to do anything about it as the rag covered my mouth and nose.

After a few seconds, I was enveloped in black.

I woke up in my underwear tied with rope to a wooden chair in a white room. I faced an open window. The sun was in my eyes and I had to squint to see. From what little I could determine, I couldn't see behind me, the room was empty. White walls, white blinding sun, and me.

"Hello?" I croaked, weakly.

Even though my greeting was barely above a whisper, I could hear a faint echo. My guess was right; the room was devoid of furniture.

"Hey, c'mon, hello!" I shouted, or did my best to shout.

I waited for a response that didn't come.

My bladder, full of last night's beer and scotch, started to press hard and I knew I wouldn't be able to hold back the flow much longer.

"Hey, it's going to get pretty messy in here in about a minute!" I shouted.

I felt my underwear go damp.

"Aw, Jesus," I said.

The floodgates opened and the urine soaked my underwear and ran down my legs. After a few seconds, a puddle formed under the chair, spread, and reached my bare feet. It took at least a full ninety seconds to empty my bladder. The puddle spread out beneath me and crept toward the walls.

The floor was slightly uneven.

"Satisfied?" I yelled.

Apparently not, as my request fell on deaf ears.

I suddenly felt ill. Last night's beer and scotch leftovers didn't want to stay put. I rocked the chair sideways until I fell over on my left side. I hit the floor hard, turned my face toward it and vomited up a vile liquid mess.

When my stomach was empty, I dry heaved for a few seconds until control returned. I inched the chair away from the mess with my shoulder.

"Hey, I'm not cleaning this!" I shouted.

The door opened and three men walked in. They wore suits and had the look of hired muscle.

"A little too late," I said.

They walked toward me. I had a good view of their shoes. Highly polished, black wingtips. The shoe of choice for organized crime soldiers.

One of them kicked me in the chin with

his shiny wingtip. "Nobody said you could fucking talk," he said.

I woke up naked in a backyard shower stall that was designed to rinse off after coming out of the pool. Three walls made of concrete, a showerhead on the back wall. The pool was shaped like an S, with a deep and shallow end. Lush gardens surrounded the pool. A massive brick barbecue pit sat off to the left. A woman in a bikini sunbathed on a recliner near the pool. If she noticed me, she didn't care that a naked stranger occupied the shower.

The three wingtips faced me from just outside the shower stall. One of them held a garden hose with a high-velocity nozzle.

"Say cheese," Nozzle Holder said and turned on the water.

The blast of ice-cold water hit me in the chest like a kick and knocked me against the cement wall.

"Ain't got no soap," Nozzle sneered. "So sorry."

I covered my genitals from the spray and sank to my knees. Nozzle Holder took pleasure in his work as he aimed for my face to try to get me to uncover my genitals. I turned and gave him my back. The water stung, but not like a high-powered blast to the balls.

"That's enough, he's clean," another wingtip said.

The water stopped. I slowly turned around. Past the three wingtips, the woman in the recliner hadn't moved a muscle.

A wingtip tossed me a white terrycloth pool robe. "Put it on," he said.

I put the robe on and tied the belt. "Now what?" I said.

"We go see the man," another wingtip said.

The three wingtips escorted me past the pool, where the reclining woman had yet to move, and into the house through sliding glass doors. I said house, I meant mansion. We walked through a long hallway of polished oak floors to a door. One of the wingtips opened the door and shoved me through it.

It was the room I had occupied earlier.

Someone had gone to a great deal of trouble to clean it up and done a thorough job. Not a spot remained on the gleaming oak floor. A chair rested in the center of the room.

"Sit," a wingtip commanded.

I went to the chair and sat. "Now what?"

"Hands behind your back," the wingtip said.

I placed my hands behind my back and the wingtip cuffed my left wrist to the slat in the chair. He used two more sets of cuffs to lock each of my legs to a chair leg.

"This isn't because you're afraid of me?" I said.

The wingtips ignored me.

No sense of humor.

We waited.

"Sorry about the mess earlier," I said. "But I warned you guys ahead of time."

We waited some more. Obviously, my wingtipped hosts weren't big on small talk, or any talk at all for that matter.

They stood like statues, ignored me, and kept a close watch on the door.

After awhile, I couldn't say how long as I had no watch and couldn't see the sun, the door opened. Two additional wingtips walked in. That wasn't any surprise.

From behind the two new wingtips came the sound of a motorized wheelchair and that was somewhat of a surprise.

The two new wingtips parted and stopped. From behind them the wheelchair rolled closer to me, and its occupant was none other than Eddie Crist.

That was a surprise. A major league fastball of the Nolan Ryan type surprise.

Even more surprising than coming face to

face with one of the most powerful mobsters in organized crime history was the fact that he was dying. He wasn't more than sixty-eight years old, but some form of cancer and chemo treatments had taken a major toll on his once large and powerful body.

I looked at Eddie Crist.

Eddie Crist looked at me.

He didn't speak.

I did.

"I can't wait for you to be fucking dead," I said.

The wingtip closest to me raised his hand as if to backhand me.

"No," Crist said.

The wingtip lowered his hand.

"I didn't kill your wife," Crist said.

"You had her killed," I said. "You turned my little girl into a fucking vegetable, you fucking piece of shit motherfucker. I hope . . . no, I pray that whatever cancer is eating you alive is slow and painful, the kind where you linger for months on end, rotting from the inside out, you putrid son of a bitch."

"Are you through?" Crist said.

"I'm just getting warmed up," I said.

"I didn't kill your wife," Crist said.

"You sent that goon to kill her," I said. "Explain to me the difference."

25

"I sent nobody."

"What do you got, stomach cancer?"

"Pancreas."

"Good. That's nice and slow and painful. There is a God after all, but you'll never meet him, you rancid piece of meat."

"I don't doubt that for a moment," Crist said. "But, that's neither here nor there. I had nothing to do with what happened to your wife or child."

"And I should believe a piece of shit low-life gangster motherfucker like you, why? Because you're sick and dying of cancer. Fuck you, scumbag."

Crist sighed. His two hundred pound body now weighed a buck twenty, if that. I could see his bones inside the red silk robe he wore. He braced his hands on the arms of the wheelchair and slowly got to his feet.

"You got cancer bad, huh," I said. "Good, because if God has . . ."

Crist slapped me across the face with the bony side of his right hand. It stung like hell and spun my head around.

When my bell stopped ringing, Crist lowered himself back into the wheelchair. "You used to be a good cop," he said. "One of the best. The only one who ever got close to me. Now you're nothing but a drunken good-for-nothing bum."

26

"Have your goons free my hand and legs and I'll save God the trouble of slow cooking your rotten ass," I said.

"We'll talk later," Crist said. "After."

Crist pushed a button on the arm of his wheelchair and started to roll away from me. "After what?" I said.

Crist rolled to the door and out of the room.

"After what?" I yelled after him.

Crist turned a corner and I lost sight of him.

"Was it something I said?" I yelled at the empty, open door.

Three wingtips surrounded me.

"What do you goons want?" I said.

They bent at the knees and picked me up by the seat of the chair.

"We go for a ride now," a wingtip said.

4

The wingtips handcuffed my left wrist to the brass headboard of a queen-size bed in an otherwise empty bedroom. The bedroom was located somewhere on the second floor of the Crist mansion.

They took the robe, leaving me naked.

They left three bedpans.

They set a small lamp on the floor beside the door and turned it on.

They left without saying a word.

I heard a key lock the door.

I sat up as best I could against the brass headboard. The mattress was void of sheets. The pillows were bare, but then so was I. On the floor within reaching distance was a green wool blanket of the type used by the military.

Would I need it? The room was comfortable enough at the moment. The open window allowed for fresh air and a slight breeze. Outside was about seventy-five degrees. After dark, that number would be around sixty.

I tried stretching to reach the blanket with my right hand, grabbed it, and flipped it onto the mattress beside the bedpans.

Three bedpans. One to urinate in, another to defecate in, the third for vomiting.

A handcuffed wrist, a locked door, and pretty soon I would require all three.

For the moment, there wasn't a hell of a lot to do, so I made myself comfortable and stared at the white ceiling until my eyes closed.

Thirteen years ago, I was part of a federal task force investigating organized crime. I was a detective with the rank of sergeant in the Special Crimes Division. My partner Walter Grimes and I were the only non-FBI in the task force. We were selected because we knew the Crist crime family, had busted several members over the years, and didn't have a problem taking our orders from the feds.

You'd be surprised how many do.

The task force focused on the war raging inside organized crime. It happens every fifteen years or so, when a Gotti type rolls in with fire in his balls. A year of my time was spent on that task force. We had charts like those you see in the movies of bosses with diagrams to their soldiers. We had videotapes, phone taps, informants, the works.

We just didn't have anything with which to charge Eddie Crist.

Walt got sick. He took his son fishing one weekend in the spring. He was bitten by a mosquito. He came down with a mysterious, but toxic staph infection. He recovered, but it took six weeks, three of which were spent hospitalized.

While Walt was recovering, I stumbled upon the first real break in the case against the Crist crime family.

Dead bosses were popping up like toast all around town and the coast. The word was Crist had had enough and wanted peace. The way to make peace in a mob war is to kill off anybody who is against your peace proposal.

Crist was smart. He knew the FBI had a jacket on each and every member of his family and organization. He imported talent from the old country. Stone-cold killers in wingtips and silk suits.

Besides smart, Crist was careful.

He used his son, Michael, to make all arrangements. Driving his own car, Michael drove to the airport where he would meet with the imported talent at various coffee shops inside the terminal. Crist knew that even if Michael was followed, there was little to nothing the feds could do about a public meeting inside an airport.

Walt was still in the hospital one morning while I was staking out the Crist mansion from my car atop the hill that overlooks his grounds. With binoculars, I watched Michael drive off the grounds in his little blue sports car.

I decided to tag along.

The ride led to the airport. I parked and followed him inside, where he sat at a terminal coffee shop and met with an imported button man. I watched their conversation from the safety of the terminal until they parted ways.

They didn't make me on their way out.

I tagged the button man to his rental car and ran his plates. After that, things fell into place quickly. He had a ninety-day visa and was staying in a rented house in the suburbs. He made frequent trips to the airport to meet Michael. I took the information to the task force in the FBI.

We set up a sting.

With the cooperation of the airport, every coffee shop, bar, and restaurant inside the terminal was staffed with a minimum of two agents as waiters. It took a week and three meetings between Michael and the button man to get the goods on them.

They met at the coffee shop in the west wing of the airport. A high-ranking under-boss was the target. The man refused to back down on his takeover of the Hispanic drug market in the city. Crist made him an offer, but he turned a deaf ear.

Mistake.

The contract was written.

We staked out the underboss. He liked to play the ponies. The hit was to take place at the racetrack during the featured race when the crowd was in a frenzy and no one would see a thing. The underboss had his people with him, but that posed no problem for a pro. It wasn't hard to worm your way through the bodies and shoot the underboss in the back of the head, then disappear in the scattering masses.

We pinched the button man minutes before he completed his task. We pegged him for seven hits and threatened him with life without parole, if he lived past his first month in federal prison.

The feds offered him a deal.

Cough up Michael Crist and fly home on the next plane out of the country.

See, if you got Michael, you got Eddie.

Three weeks later, while the button man

sat in a safe house and spilled his guts to federal prosecutors, a bomb went off in the kitchen and blew everybody to kingdom come.

I wasn't there.

I was visiting my partner on his last day in the hospital. While I brought Walt up to speed on the investigation, a man sent by Crist broke into my house to give Carol a warning meant for me. Back off, he was to say.

He raped and murdered her instead.

He turned my five-year-old daughter into a living, breathing house plant.

When the smoke cleared, I crawled inside a bottle of scotch and called it home ever since.

My eyes slowly opened.

My throat was as dry as an emery board. The sweats had begun. A thirst was building in my throat that nothing but alcohol would quench. My hands shook a little.

A while later, they shook a lot.

A little while after that, the bed was soaked in my stale sweat. I urinated into one bedpan and defecated into another. I vomited into the third, then diarrhea set in, followed by dehydration.

By nightfall, I was in full-blown cold turkey detox. I could barely stand the smell of myself and tried to keep my nose buried in the pillow. I pissed on the bed rather than move. There is something very humbling about urinating in your own diarrhea.

A little more time passed.

I had the shakes so bad, my eyeballs rattled. I was cold and sweating at the same time and covered my body up to my neck with the wool blanket. After a time, I had to remove it because it soaked up so much sweat, I couldn't stand the weight on my body.

I wanted to scream, to shake, rattle, and roll. I kept my mouth shut and didn't utter a word. I didn't want to give Crist the satisfaction of hearing me beg for booze.

I tried to focus, but of course that's impossible when every pore in your body is craving a drink so badly, you'd sell your soul for just one shot.

Or two.

A little while after the shakes kicked in, I fell asleep or passed out. I'm not sure which, but it didn't matter. I went in and out for a while, saw or heard a man hovering over me and heard him speak.

Then I felt a needle go into my right arm just below the forearm. I opened my eyes and saw the IV bag above my head.

The man was giving me fluids. A mixture

of water-based electrolytes like in the hospital. For dehydration. And cramps.

My eyes closed again and when they opened, the man and his IV were gone.

Sunlight was filtering in through the window, low against the wall when I came around. It was early morning, somewhere around seven or so. The worst of it was over. I had nothing left in me to sweat out. My hands still shook, though not as pronounced, and my nerves were still wired.

The door opened again and the man from the night before walked in, accompanied by three wingtips. The man wore a suit and carried another IV bag. He stopped at the bed, while the wingtips stayed in the background.

"Well," he said. "You've come through the worst of it in one piece. I'm going to give you an IV and after that, some soup and crackers. I'll have a small table brought in so you can sit and eat while the bedding is changed."

"And if I take this IV and shove it up your nose, then what?" I said.

"My three associates here will take measures to correct your behavior and that won't be pleasant," the man said.

"Then I guess I'll eat soup," I said.

My body absorbed eight ounces of IV

fluids. I asked for a cigarette and the man nodded to the wingtips. One of them stepped forward, gave me a cigarette, and lit it with a gold Zippo.

"So what's your stake in this?" I asked the man.

"My name is Doctor Steven Richards. I am Mr. Crist's personal physician. I have been for twenty-three years. He's requested I look after you."

"Why?"

"I don't ask why, Mr. Bekker," Richards said. "I do what is asked and what is necessary."

I sucked on the cigarette. The smoke was hot in my throat and lungs. It wasn't my brand, but it got the job done. My hand steadied a little. What more could you ask from a smoke?

"Crist wanted me sober?" I said. "Why?"

"I don't know," Richards said. "But, sober you are and ready for some nourishment." He looked at a wingtip. "Bring Mr. Bekker a robe."

"What kind of soup?" I said.

"I requested beef broth with potatoes from Mr. Crist's chef," Richards said.

"Sounds yummy," I said.

Richards turned and nodded to the wingtips, then opened the door and walked out. A little while later, I ate tasteless, salt-less beef broth with potatoes and drank weak iced tea at a folding table with chair while a housekeeper changed the sheets on the bed. I was free of handcuffs, but the three wingtips stood close by and watched my every move like a hungry cat on an injured mouse.

I was the mouse.

By the time I finished the soup, crackers, and tea, the bed was changed and made and the housekeeper left without saying a word.

"The doc says for you to take a shower," a wingtip said. "And put on pajamas."

"How long am I going to be here?" I said.

"You don't talk," the wingtip said.

"Can I have some cigarettes and something to read?"

"On the bed, give me your wrist," the wingtip commanded.

A little while later, the housekeeper returned with pajamas, a fresh pack of cigarettes of my brand with matches, and a hardcover copy of the latest Leonard novel. She was accompanied by three wingtips who oversaw the dressing of the robe ceremony. She wasn't impressed enough with me to try and sneak a peek.

I couldn't exactly blame her.

I settled in to read the book and smoke a

few cigarettes. I tried to concentrate on the intricate plot lines, complex characters, and snappy dialogue of Leonard's writing, while ignoring the growing thirst in my belly.

Not easy to do when your belly is used to a quart or more of hard booze on a daily basis. I read fifty pages, smoked a few cigarettes, then set the book aside and tried to sleep for a while.

Of course, that was impossible.

I was in the home of the mobster responsible for the rape and death of my wife and the ruination of my daughter's life. He kidnapped me, forced me off the booze, and held me prisoner for reasons unknown. I wasn't treated badly, in fact just the opposite.

Crist knew that given the slightest opportunity, I would choke him to death and piss on his corpse, yet he was cordial to me, even if it was against my will.

He had an angle.

Everybody does.

So what was his?

I rolled some thoughts around in my mind. After a decade or more after the fact, what did Crist want with me now? He could have had me killed anytime he wanted and my body would never have been found. Killing me was out of the question. Why clean me up just to put me down?

Crist had cancer and that was a good thing.

Crist would be dead soon and that was an even better thing.

What did that have to do with me?

Especially now.

I fell asleep, woke up a while later, and read some more. I was on page ninety-seven when the door opened and the housekeeper, along with two wingtips, walked in. Housekeeper had a tray with grilled cheese sandwiches, French fries, and iced tea on a serving tray, the kind used for breakfast in bed.

Housekeeper spoke. "I'll be back in one hour for the tray."

I ate and read. Housekeeper returned after one hour, this time with just one wingtip. She spoke again.

"The doctor said you can eat more solid food for dinner," Housekeeper said. "What would you like?"

"Steak, medium, baked potato, corn, and pie with ice cream," I said. "Skip the iced tea. Make it a tall Coke with ice. And some rum."

Housekeeper glared at me. Maybe she was the cat's meow at keeping house, but I couldn't speak much to her sense of humor.

"Just Coke with ice," I said.

Housekeeper nodded and she and wingtips went away.

I'd gone from three bodyguards to two and finally just one. I had gained trust or wasn't seen as much of a threat. My money was on not much of a threat.

I slept, read, smoked, and slept some more.

Doctor Richards, one wingtip, and Housekeeper returned with the steak just as I awoke. I sat up ready to eat.

"Let's have a look at you first," Richards said.

The wingtip removed the cuffs and I removed the pajama top. Richards listened to my heart and lungs, took my blood pressure and pulse, and seemed satisfied I wouldn't expire while under his care.

"How long am I going to be kept here?" I asked Richards.

"I can't say," Richards said.

"What can you say?" I said.

"I can say enjoy the steak," Richards said.

I did. Immensely.

Thirty-six hours later, I got my answer.

5

The charcoal gray, silk shirt was my size and a perfect fit. So were the tan slacks and loafers. The black socks were black socks. Nothing much to say about socks no matter what they're made of.

I shaved using a disposable razor with gel type shaving cream, the kind that lathered when you rubbed it against your skin. After a shower, I dressed. I didn't feel like a new man. I felt like an old man in new clothes.

Two wingtips escorted me from the vast second floor of the mansion to the formal dining room on the north side of the first floor. From what little I could see, the first floor was furnished with the most expensive, best of everything.

Who said crime didn't pay?

Not me.

It did. And a lot.

"Where are we going?" I said to the wingtips as we walked the maze of rooms.

"We aren't going anywhere," a wingtip said. "You are having dinner with Mr. Crist."

And with that, we stopped in front of the dining room where one wingtip slid open a set of heavy mahogany double doors. "Inside," the other wingtip said.

It wasn't a request.

I went inside. They closed the doors. I looked around. The dining room was at least forty feet long by thirty feet wide. A polished mahogany table for twenty centered the room. Matching chairs completed the look. A dozen mid-floor to ceiling windows were covered by silk drapes, closed at the moment. Six mini Tiffany lamps suspended above the table glowed softly, illuminating the table and nothing else.

Two place settings occupied the table. One at the west end, the other to its left.

I sat at the left and waited. The china was the real thing, so was the silverware. The water glass and pitcher were crystal. Crist didn't skimp on the dinnerware, or much else from what I could see.

I filled my glass with water and took a sip.

Ten minutes later, the doors opened and Crist rolled in on his motorized wheelchair. Two wingtips accompanied him, one on each side. Crist rolled to his chair, turned

42

off the power, set his hands on the arms and gently stood. A wingtip pulled out the chair and Crist sat.

"Wait over there," Crist said and the wingtips walked to the window and stood watching us.

"Still want me dead?" Crist said.

"With all the passion Romeo had for Juliet," I said.

Crist chuckled softly. "I never did care much for Shakespeare," he said. Then he filled his water glass and took a sip, lowered it, and looked at me. "I'll be dead in three months, maybe four at most," he said. "How's that for a sonnet?"

"Good things come to those who wait," I said. "Isn't that how the saying goes?"

"It's how the saying goes, it isn't how life works," Crist said.

"What do you want?" I said.

Crist turned and nodded at the wingtips. One wingtip slid open the doors and a butler wheeled in a large trolley with dinner. Breaded pork chops with some kind of sauce, potatoes, corn, carrots, and asparagus in some other kind of sauce, several types of breads, and cake with coffee for dessert.

"Hungry?" Crist said.

"For information, but I'll eat," I said.

"So eat," Crist said.

I ate while Crist nibbled.

"I don't even know what a pancreas does, but it's going to kill me," Crist said.

"It's a gland that helps digestion," I said. "It's located near the stomach. Thankfully, it's one of the few cancers still left around they can't cure."

Crist stared at me for a moment.

I ate a slice of breaded pork chop.

"Bekker is what kind of name?" Crist said.

"My father was Danish," I said.

"Your mother?"

"Italian and Irish," I said. "But, I'm sure you already have a complete bio on me."

"My daughter is useless," Crist said.

"So is mine," I said.

Crist stared at me for a moment.

"Campbell is forty-two years old and spends her days lounging at the pool and nights in the city accompanied by a never-ending stream of gigolos," Crist said. "She thinks when I'm gone she will inherit all that I have, but she won't. Some is going to the Catholic Church. A great deal of it is going to family in the old country. A lot is going to the government. My daughter will have to learn to live on a million dollars a year. She can go through that in a month."

"Campbell," I said. "Like the soup?"

"Be thankful I didn't name her Progresso."

"Not that I haven't enjoyed your little story, but I don't really give a fuck about you, your daughter, or your finances," I said.

"My son was murdered by the Campo Family five years ago when they made a move on the Vegas operation," Crist said. "They shot him six times in the heart and once in the brain in his Vegas residence. He was forty years old at the time."

I didn't know that, or maybe I did and forgot. News isn't a priority when you're drunk most of the time.

"Michael was to be my successor," Crist said. "Now there isn't one."

"Regan was to be a wife, mother, and a whole person," I said. "Now she won't be one. Carol was to grow old with me. Now she won't. Am I supposed to feel sorry for you? I don't."

Crist took a sip of water, then dabbed his lips with a linen napkin. "Listen to what I have to say. When I'm done, you can leave. Just don't interrupt me until I'm done."

I shoved pork chop into my mouth and nodded.

"I make no apologies for my life," Crist said. "My father was a driver, then a runner for the Gambino family. I got my start at the age of fourteen. I was doing hits at sixteen and driving the bosses by eighteen. Now I'm sixty-eight and being eaten alive by cancer. So what?"

So what? That's what I thought, but I kept my tongue silent by filling my mouth with food.

"I have no idea how many lives I've taken, with the gun or with the drugs I peddle around college campuses and in slums," Crist continued. "I ruin families in my Vegas casinos, rip them off at my car dealerships, and force them to repay loans at forty percent interest when banks won't satisfy them. I've never involved a civilian in a family-related dispute, including yours. I never sent anybody to scare you off your investigation. For one thing, you were just a local cop who got lucky. For another, I bought and paid for judges, prosecutors, and even jury members to make sure my boy walked. You were just something I scrape off the bottom of my shoe."

Crist took another sip of water.

I ate some corn. It was pretty good.

"When I heard what happened to your wife and daughter, I was shocked," Crist continued. "For several reasons. One is that I'd never punish the wife or daughter of someone who hurt me. I'd punish that

46

someone. Two is that I never authorized anyone to scare you off. It's a ridiculous concept to me. Someone acted on their own for reasons of their own. I tried for the longest time to find out who that someone was, but they were buried so deep or were dead or so well connected that it was impossible. My son was a hothead prone to violence. I suspected he might have arranged for your home to be broken into as revenge for your involvement in the investigation. He assured me that he didn't, but I could never be positive once he was killed. Whatever you may think of me, Bekker, I'm not an animal in the woods. Your wife and daughter have bothered me all these years. I want to do something about it before I leave this world."

I took a sip of water. "Why now? Because you're dying? It won't clear your conscience."

"It's my valediction, so to speak," Crist said. "My act of contrition."

"It won't buy you a seat in heaven."

"No, but maybe I won't have to sit on the back of the bus in hell."

"So you want to do what?" I said.

"Find who murdered your wife and damaged your daughter before I take that seat on the bus," Crist said. "Even if it means my son was responsible. I have no regrets or fears for my life. I've done what I've done knowing full well my actions, but never for blood, only for business."

"You want I should clap here?" I said. "While you take a bow. If you can manage to stand, that is."

"What I want," Crist said, with dark anger in his eyes for the first time, "is for you to sober up long enough to find the man responsible for your wife's murder. After that, if you want to crawl back into a bottle and drink yourself to death, that's your business. Why didn't you just put a gun to your head and end it if you're so fucking miserable?"

"I was ending it," I said. "I just chose the slow route."

"What do you want, Bekker?" Crist said, visibly agitated. "To see me beg and crawl? Well, I can't. I can barely walk anymore."

"Oh, appealing to my sympathy now," I said.

"If I have to," Crist said. "When was the last time you saw your daughter?"

"That's none of your . . ."

"Answer the fucking question," Crist snapped.

"Couple of months," I said.

"More like seven."

"How do you know?" I said, fearing the answer.

"You are nothing but a drunk," Crist said. "Too weak to do what's right for your own daughter."

"What do you know about it?" I said.

"That state hospital she was in, your disability and wife's insurance policy barely covered her expenses," Crist said. "When they transferred her to the private facility she's in now, do you really think Social Security covers the bills? Eight thousand a month? Left to you, your daughter would be living in a state facility where they'd stick her in a room for sixty years and forget about her."

I stared at Crist.

He read my face.

"Every month for ten years, my accountants send a check to the private facility," Crist said. "I made arrangements for her for the rest of her life so you can drink yourself to death and not worry she won't be cared for, but if you ask me, I'd say you don't give a fuck. About your daughter. About your dead wife. About yourself."

Crist turned and looked at the wingtips. "Send in my lawyer."

One wingtip went to the door, opened it, and motioned to someone outside. A moment later, a tall man of about sixty walked in with a briefcase. He came to the table, nodded to Crist, and took a chair directly opposite me.

"This is Frank Kagan," Crist said. "He's my personal attorney who handles all my family matters."

I nodded to Kagan.

Kagan opened the briefcase and withdrew a document. He perched reading glasses on his nose, scanned the documents, and said, "Mr. Crist has authorized in his will a provision for the lifelong care of Regan Marie Bekker, your daughter. Her expenses in their entirety are to be paid in full on the first of every month until the time of her death. A provision for her death is included with an amendment for the wishes of her father, John Bekker. Do you understand what I have just read to you?"

"Yes," I said.

Kagan looked at Crist. "Mr. Crist?"

"Find who killed your wife," Crist said to me. "Even if it was my son, I need to know. I don't want to die with this hanging over my head."

"I haven't been a cop for a long time," I said.

"That doesn't matter," Crist said. "You're still connected. I'll give you whatever you need, but you will do this, if not for yourself or me, then for your daughter. You owe her that much at least. Your wife, too."

I stared at Crist.

I nodded my head.

"No fucking booze," Crist said. "Not one goddamn drop until you find this man and bring him to me. I find you drinking, I'll have your pinkies removed with garden shears. Understood?"

"Yes."

Crist turned to Kagan.

Kagan removed another file from the briefcase and slid it across the table to me. "Mr. Crist has arranged and paid for a state-issued private investigator's license and pistol permit in the name of John Bekker. A contract has been drawn up whereby Mr. Crist is employing the services of John Bekker to investigate the death of Carol Bekker twelve years earlier. Mr. Bekker is to be handsomely compensated for his employment in addition to expenses. Employment is to begin immediately. Mr. Crist expects that Mr. Bekker report to him any and all findings relevant to his employment as they occur immediately, and he is to take orders only from Mr. Crist until said employment is terminated. Is this understood? My office is to be your liaison to Mr.

Crist. Is that understood?"

"Yes," I said. "On all counts."

Kagan slid a pen across the table. "Sign here."

I signed.

I looked at the license and pistol permit.

"Amazing what fucking money can buy," Crist said. "When people are willing to be bribed."

I looked at the expense check and retainer for my services.

I was now gainfully employed to investigate the murder of my wife by the very man I believed to have murdered her.

I looked at Crist.

Crist chuckled. "Life is one big ironic fucking surprise, isn't it?" he said.

6

I sat in my rusty lawn chair, sipped coffee from a mug, and stared at the ocean. A full pot of black coffee rested on the card table beside me. I didn't have the shakes anymore. I didn't even have the urge to drink, but who knew for how long? I knew my system was in shock and that it would wear off soon enough.

Then we'll see.

How strong I am.

How willing I am to fight.

I grabbed my smokes and lit one off a paper match.

Said another way, how weak I really was.

Next to the coffee pot was the shoebox I kept under the bed. I looked at the shoebox. I knew I had to open it, but not yet.

Waves crashed on the beach and against the rocky shoreline. The tide was coming in and with each break, the waves rumbled like thunder.

I looked at the shoebox again.

It hadn't moved.

Did I expect it to?

Heartache is like heartburn, but without the little blue pill to cure it.

I opened the shoebox.

Waves crashed on the beach. I puffed on my cigarette. Gulls battled each other for scraps of food in the sand. I withdrew the yellow, frayed newspaper clipping from the shoebox.

It was the first account in the papers of a cop's wife who was raped and brutally beaten, finally strangled to death while her five-year-old daughter watched in shock.

The second story was about the cop who suffered a complete breakdown upon hearing the news. How it took six officers in his own department to prevent him from entering the crime scene of his own home.

Another story linked the murder to an ongoing organized crime investigation. Lawyers for the Crist Organization denied knowledge of the murder, claiming a lawsuit against the police if it was insinuated.

A story covering Carol's funeral. Police in dress blues, my captain standing by my side in a show of support. The department band playing as Carol's coffin was lowered into the ground by six officers, one of them being my partner, Walter Grimes. Me seated in a folding chair, the only expression on my face empty shock.

Coverage of the captain's press conference where he vigorously claimed the person responsible for Carol's death would be hunted with every resource in the department until found, arrested, and convicted.

A story about my complete breakdown a few months later, leading to my disability retirement from the department.

A follow-up story on the captain's press conference months later where he announced it was time to move on, but the investigation would remain open and active.

I set the clippings aside, filled the mug, lit another cigarette, and pulled out copies of police reports.

The first was written by the uniformed officers responding to a neighbor's 911 call. The neighbor stated she heard a woman screaming from inside my house. The officers, Patrolman Ronson and Corporal Olsen, found my front door open, drew their weapons and flashlights, and entered my house. They found Carol on the bed and my daughter in the bathtub. They knew to touch nothing and immediately called Homicide. They removed Regan to their patrol car.

Homicide detective Art Stiles, who I knew quite well, and his partner, a first-year homicide detective named Dave Peterson with six years on the job as patrolman, arrived at my house fifteen minutes later. They immediately sent for the ME and the CSI squad. They debated with my captain by phone about who should be the one to call me. The captain volunteered. He had to make six or seven calls to locate me in Walt's hospital room. He told me there was an emergency at my home. I arrived forty-five minutes later not knowing what to expect, just that it would be bad.

It always is when the captain makes the call.

Art Stiles' report stated that when he and Peterson arrived on scene, Carol was on her back on our bed. She was naked. Her hair was still wet from the shower she was taking when the intruder attacked. She died hard, fighting for her life and the life of our daughter the way only a mother could. The intruder punched her in the face several times before dragging her to the bed where he raped and choked her until she died from a broken windpipe. Regan had been playing with her toys on the bedroom floor when the intruder arrived. She hid under the bed, then crawled into the bathtub afterward.

Art took preliminary photos of Carol and the house with his digital camera. He and Peterson didn't begin a search for evidence until after the scene was cleared by the ME and Forensics.

Medical Examiner Andrew Viceroy, a man I knew for half my tenure with the department, arrived fifteen minutes before I did. He'd attended Carol's Christmas party the last three years and was said to have wept as he made his initial examination. He later wrote upon autopsy that Carol's throat had been crushed by strangulation, the cause of death. Blood was found under her fingernails on the right hand. Strands of hair were found in her left hand and on the bed. She had been raped hard, Viceroy explained in his report. Carol's vagina was torn and bruised by forced penetration, but void of seminal secretions. So too was the bed, carpet, and Carol's body. The intruder either didn't ejaculate or had a vasectomy. Condoms leave traces of fluids behind and there were none. Viceroy didn't write in his report that it was possible the intruder used an object to rape my wife, but we all thought it, if we didn't say it. The forensics team searched every square inch of my house and grounds for the object without finding it, whatever it may have been.

The CSI forensics team of six, headed by supervisor Matt Henin, took my house apart searching for evidence. They DNA-typed the intruder's hair and blood, but a computer match was never found. They found no fingerprints or footprints around the house. They did find the intruder's entry point. Carol turned the house alarm system off to allow our cat Cuddles access to the backyard. She did so every morning at nine and turned the system back on at eleven when Cuddles returned inside for her nap on the sofa. A ten-foot-high picket fence surrounded our sixty-by-eighty-foot back-yard. The intruder scaled the fence and entered through the kitchen. It was logical to conclude the intruder knew Carol's habits, what she did when, and a backlog of system reports from the alarm company backed that up. We were under observation, no doubt. For how long was anybody's guess.

I arrived at my house to find six patrol cars and a dozen uniforms on my lawn. Captain James Jonas, a long-time friend as well as supervisor, broke the news to me as best he could. How do you tell a man his wife has just been murdered and the only witness is his five-year-old daughter? I don't remember.

I don't remember losing control. I don't remember being restrained or busting the jaw of one of the officers restraining me. I don't remember having to be tased, cuffed, and shoved into an ambulance. I don't remember being shot up with tranquilizers by an EMT. I don't remember being transported to the hospital, put in restraints, and waking up screaming my wife's name in the middle of the night.

It probably was a blessing.

Some things are just too painful to remember.

It's easier to forget them inside a bottle.

I set the reports on the card table, wiped my eyes dry, and went into the trailer. I fixed a couple of smoked turkey sandwiches on club rolls, grabbed a bag of chips and a can of Coke, and returned to my chair.

I ate the first sandwich and watched the tide cover the rocks. Between sandwiches, I munched on chips and sipped soda from the can. I took a break to smoke a cigarette and glanced into the shoebox.

What remained were a couple of reports by my former partner, Walter Grimes. He requested a temporary assignment to Homicide and spent several unfruitful months working the case.

I didn't hold his lack of results against

him. The FBI and their special task force drew blanks across the board, so what were the locals supposed to achieve?

I heard a soft noise, looked down, and a mutt cat was sniffing around my leg. He or she was a stray, feral and hungry. I ripped off a piece of turkey from the second sandwich and tossed it beside the mutt. It gobbled up the turkey without bothering to chew. I tossed it another piece, then reached for Walt's reports.

While I sat in a psych ward under sedation for weeks on end, Walt and the FBI task force left no stone unturned. Every ranking member of Organized Crime was brought in for questioning and released when results were fruitless. Every local and two-bit thief, junkie, and gangbanger got the same treatment on the outside chance Carol's death was unrelated to the Crist investigation. Every hit man and contract killer was looked into, home and abroad, without results. Every rock was looked under, every snitch brought in for questioning.

Months passed. The investigation stalled. The FBI was forced to move on to bigger and better things, like homegrown terrorism. Walt had to return to his regular duties in Special Crimes.

I guess after fruitless months of hard work, Carol wasn't so special anymore.

The cat meowed at my feet. I tossed it another piece of turkey and when it turned to eat it, I could see she was a female.

"I don't suppose you have a name," I said to the cat.

She ate her turkey.

Who was I to question her authority?

I went into the trailer for a notepad, pen, and a mug of coffee. When I returned, the cat was on the card table, eating my turkey sandwich sans the bread. I sat, sipped my coffee, lit a cigarette, and the cat didn't pay me the slightest bit of attention.

"This is a bad start to our relationship," I told the cat.

She ate turkey.

I drank coffee and smoked my cigarette.

I looked at the blank page in the notebook on my lap. I had no words with which to fill the page. No list of suspects. No list of hard evidence or facts to show me the way. Nobody to interview, see, or tail. Not even a desperate fact-finding reach in the dark for a starting point.

Police work is like that most of the time. Cases get solved and bad guys get put away mostly because the vast majority of criminals are stupid.

That's the secret to being a successful cop. Go after the stupidest in the bunch and more often than not, they're the guilty or can lead you to the guilty.

I avoided writing on the page what I knew must be written.

I heard the cat purring. She was licking her face with her paw. Half the turkey sandwich was consumed. She stopped licking her face long enough to look at me. Her eyes were smoky gray.

I went into the trailer, returned with a saucer of milk, and set it on the card table. The cat lapped it up.

I wrote on the page, *Interview Crist concerning his son's involvement in the murder of Carol Bekker.*

7

I'm a big believer in doing nothing when nothing is called for. As any good detective knows, doing something just for the sake of doing it can and often does upset the apple-cart. Many a criminal walked out of court a free man because an overzealous cop over-stepped boundaries when he should have laid back and waited for the criminal to screw up on his own and hand him a con-viction.

In my case, doing nothing was a process developed from years of police work. I found, as someone with insomnia often does, that the way to sleep, or in my case think, is to try not to sleep or think, and sleep or thoughts will come.

I watched the cat lick milk from the sau-cer.

I watched the waves on the beach.

I wrote, *Who benefited by removing me from the investigation?*

I removed my wallet from a back pocket and looked at my expired driver's license. Would I, at my age, have to take a driving test to renew it?

I wrote, *Who benefited so much they would risk the FBI and police department hounding them like dogs on a squirrel?*

I went inside and returned with a small tin box. It had a lock, but it long ago broke. I opened the box and removed the documents. Years ago, while I was in a blind drunk breakdown, Carol's sister, Janet, stepped up to the plate and took charge. She arranged for the sale of our house, paid off the bank, and deposited the equity into an account for me. Thirty-seven thousand dollars and change. Sitting there for ten years. I'd forgotten all about it.

Another document was the paid mortgage on the trailer. I used insurance money for that and have lived on my forty percent disability check ever since. It wasn't much, but you don't need much when all you do is sit in a lawn chair and drink the days away.

I looked at the cat. She was curled into a ball, sound asleep on the card table.

I wrote, *Who was/is smart enough to outsmart the FBI and police department?*

There was a checkbook with eighty-seven dollars and thirteen cents in the tin box.

The last entry was nine years and seven months ago. Was the account even open and valid anymore?

There was the title to my car. I hadn't seen it in a decade. I wondered what happened to it, tried to remember, and gave that one up.

I picked up my bank account book again and stared at it for a minute. I set it back in the tin box and wrote, *Whoever benefited the most killed my wife.*

I heard a noise and looked down the beach at Oz as he walked toward me with a six-pack of beer in his left hand.

I lit a fresh cigarette and waited for Oz to arrive.

"Where'd you get the cat?" Oz said as he took his seat.

"It sort of got me," I said.

"You fed it," Oz said as he set the six-pack between us. "You never get rid of it."

"I think it's a her," I said.

"Her," Oz said as he twisted off the cap on a beer and took a sip.

"Oz," I said. "Do you own a car?"

"Car?" Oz said with a wrinkled brow. "I haven't been behind the wheel of a car since . . . a long time. Why?"

"Some things I need to do for my daughter," I said. "I'll need a car."

"Got a license?"

"No."

"My kid brother is a supervisor over at DMV," Oz said. "I'll ask him what he can do for you tomorrow at the pay phone. You might have to take a cab to get there."

"Thanks, Oz."

"Sure."

The cat rolled over and covered her eyes with her paws.

"That why you was gone a few days, this thing with your daughter?" Oz said.

"Yeah."

"And why you ain't reached for a beer by now?"

"Yeah."

"Everybody need a reason," Oz said.

I nodded.

In the notebook, I wrote, *Carol was killed for a reason. Find the reason and find whoever killed her.*

"Game on tonight," Oz said. "Giants and St. Louis. That kid pitching for the Giants."

"The skinny kid with the fastball?"

Oz nodded.

"Want something to eat?"

"I could nosh."

I fired up the coals.

Often reason and motive aren't the same thing. I learned that as a beat cop a long time ago. A man who is broke has a reason to rob a bank, but isn't motivated to do so because he isn't desperate enough to risk prison. A man who is broke and has a wife he loves who needs expensive cancer treatments and they have no insurance is motivated enough to risk that prison term.

Earlier, when I walked to town to pick up the turkey and bread, I bought some nice link sausage perfect for the grill. I tossed on the sausage and some potatoes to bake and we watched the sun start to sink lower in the sky.

The cat suddenly awoke as the aroma of cooking sausage caught her attention.

"Feed her again, she never gonna leave," Oz said.

"I know," I said.

I rolled out the TV. We ate sausage and baked potatoes while the skinny kid on the Giants made fools of the Cardinals with his fastball. I cut up a hunk of sausage for the cat and she ate it off the card table. Oz drank the entire six-pack while I stayed with coffee.

At the seventh inning stretch, I popped a bag of popcorn and brought it and the bottle of scotch I had under the sink out to the card table. Oz drank the scotch. I drank coffee. We both ate the popcorn and gave some to the cat.

Son of a bitch if she didn't eat it.

8

I called Frank Kagan from the pay phone outside the diner where I'd just had breakfast. A pleasant-sounding woman asked who was calling and when I told her John Bekker, she told me to hold for Mr. Kagan.

I held. She didn't tell me I would be holding for seven minutes, during which time I smoked a cigarette to the filter.

"Mr. Bekker," Kagan said when he finally came on the line. "What can I do for you?"

"I'd like to see Mr. Crist," I said.

"When?"

"Possibly tomorrow."

"Purpose."

"You need to know that?"

"I need to know anything and everything that concerns Mr. Crist," Kagan said. "Or might incriminate him."

"You mean besides the phone book thick FBI file on him?" I said.

I wasn't sure if Kagan chuckled or not.

He may have just been clearing his throat.

"I have some preliminary questions for Mr. Crist," I said. "Concerning his son. I need a starting point and I can only get that from Crist himself."

"Not tomorrow," Kagan said. "Day after. Mr. Crist has an appointment with his doctors today. I can set up a meeting for ten A.M. the day after."

"I'll see you then, Mr. Kagan," I said.

After I hung up, I went back into the diner for change, returned to the pay phone, and dialed the number for the local cabstand. I had time to drink a takeout container of coffee and smoke two cigarettes before the cab finally arrived.

The ride to the DMV took forty-five minutes. I tipped the driver twenty-five percent of the meter. He drove away happy.

If I had taken a number and got on the license renewal line, it would have been an hour before it was my turn. There would have been forms to fill out, tests to take, and appointments to make. Instead, I went to the customer service window and told the woman I had an appointment with Oz's younger brother, Albert.

Albert was a handsome man of about sixty. He wore rimless glasses, had skin the color of smooth coffee, and liquid brown

70

eyes. His office wasn't much, but the state didn't provide much. Albert had to make do with what he had. His pride in his work was obvious by his neat as a pin desk and appearance.

"I have to admit that I was a bit surprised when my brother called me," Albert said. "We generally don't speak much anymore. Since his . . . accident. How is he these days?"

"About what you would expect," I said.

"Yes," Albert said. "Well, anyway, I checked your history, Mr. Bekker, and usually when someone's license has been expired as long as yours has, a driving test is required. In your case, a decorated police veteran, I think I can make an exception."

"Thank you," I said.

We looked at each other.

"From what I understand, you take care of my brother," Albert said. "If you didn't feed him, he probably wouldn't eat. He'd probably be dead by now."

"He's had a rough time," I said.

"From what I've read, so have you," Albert said.

"Maybe that's why we're friends."

"I've thought about visiting him, but . . ." Albert removed his glasses for a moment to wipe them on a cloth he kept in his desk. "I

71

was following him home that day from our mother's house after a family gathering. I . . . witnessed the accident."

Albert returned the glasses to his nose and looked at me.

"A visit might do him some good," I said.

"Yes," Albert said.

We sat for a moment thinking the same thing, that the accident didn't destroy their family, the booze did.

I left Albert with my new driver's license and walked seven blocks to a used car dealership that advertised the best prices in town. I doubted that, but walked the lot unobserved until a salesman spotted me and emerged from the office wearing his best smile. He had capped teeth.

"Good morning, friend, and welcome to . . ." he said.

"That seven-year-old Grand Marquis," I said. "I want snow tires on it."

"Snow tires?" he said. "We don't sell tires here, friend, just cars."

"That explains why the tires are capped and bald," I said. "Knock the price down one thousand and I'll take the car."

"You don't want to test drive it?"

"I trust you," I said. "Friend."

I went into debt for sixty-five hundred dollars and drove the Marquis to the first VIP

72

store I came to, went in, and had four snow tires put on. The man in Parts looked at me as if I had two heads, but happily took my six hundred dollars.

From the VIP store, I drove around a bit to get the feel of the Marquis. It handled well, had the ride of a big car, which meant no sharp turns, but it had plenty of power and got fairly good mileage. The tires were noisy, though.

My next stop was a cell phone store. My last cell phone was for department use and the size of a brick. It had a retractable antenna for reception. A kid of about nineteen with acne placed a phone the size of my thumb in my hand and told me to try out the special features. I asked for something a little bigger without the features. I doubted I would be texting, playing video games, or downloading tunes anytime soon. I settled for a cigarette pack–size phone that took digital photos. It came with a car charger and I plugged it into the cigarette lighter as I drove to my next stop.

At the bank branch where Janet deposited the money from my house-sale, I happily learned that the thirty-seven thousand dollars was now worth fifty-one thousand thanks to some rollover interest rate I didn't understand. The assistant branch manager guided me in opening a new checking account, depositing Crist's check into it, establishing direct deposit for my disability checks, and securing a Visa card.

From breakfast to lunch, my life was suddenly much more complicated. I was back in the system, no longer off grid. I wasn't sure yet how I felt about that. The system has a way of catching up to you.

By twelve-thirty, I was ready for lunch and found a small diner off the beaten path on Main Street. I went in and chose a booth by a window. My waitress, a woman of about thirty, wrinkled her brow when I asked if they had a phone book I could borrow. I might as well have been asking for dinosaur bones. I ate without the phone book, but I did read the local newspaper I purchased from the machine outside the diner.

I returned to the Marquis and smoked a cigarette while I made the first ever call from my new cell phone.

"Walter Grimes, please," I said to the desk sergeant when she answered the phone.

"Lieutenant Grimes is unavailable today," the desk sergeant, a no-nonsense sounding woman, said. "May I ask who is calling?"

"Sergeant John Bekker," I said. "The

lieutenant and I were once partners. Could you tell him I called."

"John Bekker?" the desk sergeant said.

"Yes."

"This is Valery Greene. I was Valery Herman at the time. I was a rookie when you were assigned here. I'm sure you don't remember me, but Walt and others speak fondly of you quite often."

I didn't remember Valery Herman-Greene, but I said, "You've done well to make sergeant, Valery. Congratulations."

"Thanks, Sergeant," Valery said. "Do you want the lieutenant to call you back?"

"Yes," I said. I looked at the little card that had the cell phone number written on it and recited it to her. "Tell him he can call anytime."

"I will," Valery said. "Maybe you should stop by the station sometime."

"That's my plan," I said.

I smoked another cigarette while I wrote a check for the Marquis. Paid in full. I drove around to find a post office and sent the payment on its way.

After that, I had nothing else to do and drove home in my new, seven-year-old Marquis.

9

The three quarters of a mile stretch of sand to my trailer was oftentimes soaked, soft, and a problem even for the kids who rode their ATV's across the beach. Today the sand was dry and posed no problem for the beastly snow tires on the Marquis.

The cat woke up from her nap where she had taken up residency on the card table when I exited the Marquis and walked to my trailer.

I scratched her head and she meowed.

On the drive home, I passed a pet store, stopped, and picked up a flea collar. I went into the trailer and returned to the cat with a plate of turkey and a saucer of milk. While she ate, I attached the collar around her neck.

"If you got 'em, we'll both feel better if you wear this," I told her.

The cat lapped up the milk and showed no resistance to the collar. Happy that she was happy, I changed into a pair of shorts and walked barefoot down to the water.

I waded in to my ankles. The water was cold, but not so cold I couldn't stand it, so I stood looking out at the ocean. The tide was low. The waves were punchless. In a few hours, that would change, but for now I stood and watched the blue ocean and enjoyed the salt sea air on my face.

Like I said, I'm a great believer in doing nothing when nothing is called for.

I thought about having a beer, but I knew that was a dangerous road to travel. One beer wouldn't quench a ten-year thirst. Best to stay thirsty.

I thought about Walt. He used to visit me sometimes, then he stopped. When did he make lieutenant? He, as well as I, would be ripe for retirement about now. How long would he stick it out? Thirty for the full one hundred percent of his pension? Probably. He wasn't that far from it right now, but I doubted pension was his motivating factor.

I thought about my daughter.

Crist was wrong when he said I hadn't seen her in seven months. The last time I saw Regan was twelve years ago when she was just five. The shell of a mind that occupied her body would never be Regan again.

I thought about my wife. Carol would be forty-five years old had she lived. What would she look like? Would her face still be firm and wrinkle free? Would her waist still be ten inches smaller than her bust? Would she still laugh as much? Cry as much? Love me as much?

Or would we be just another middle-aged couple with a teenage daughter we couldn't control?

Some gulls behind me argued over some scraps. I turned around and watched them for a moment. A victor emerged from the pack and flew off with the prize, a dead fish that floated in on a soft wave.

I walked over to Oz's trailer where he was napping on the sofa. He awoke after several hard raps on the door and poked his head out. He blinked a few times and said, "Bekker, man, something wrong?"

"Your brother came through on the license," I said. "I bought a car."

Oz came out and looked down the beach. "What is that?"

"Grand Marquis."

"That's an old man car, isn't it?"

"Sometimes the shoe fits. Listen, I have to run an errand. Make sure you eat something."

"How long you gonna be?"

"Few hours, maybe more."

"I won't be hungry till then, anyway."

"I'll pick up a couple of pizzas," I said.

"Extra cheese and sausage."

"Garlic rolls?"

"Go without saying."

"Later, then," I said.

At my trailer, I scratched the cat behind her ears and she rolled over on the card table and purred.

"You need a name," I told the cat.

She purred her response.

"I'll think on it," I said.

The cat rolled over again, sat up, and looked at me.

I used my key to unlock the door and entered the trailer. I paused to look around. I wasn't much of a housekeeper. In fact, I wasn't a housekeeper at all. A small bomb would have done less damage than my lack of cleaning skills.

In the bedroom, I foraged through the closet for something decent to wear. Hard to do when most of your wardrobe is a decade or more outdated. I found a light-weight gray pinstripe that, if not in style, wasn't so far gone I couldn't be buried in it.

I stripped and shaved carefully at the tiny bathroom sink. My hands didn't shake. A bonus when scraping your neck with a razor-sharp blade. After a shower, I dug out a clean white shirt from the bottom drawer of my dresser, put on the suit with a pair of black shoes, and locked the trailer door.

"We'll eat when I get back," I told the cat. She meowed.

10

I drove one hour west before turning north for another thirty minutes. It was dinnertime in the suburbs when I pulled the Marquis into a driveway and parked next to a Taurus station wagon.

I got out and looked at the house.

Not much had changed in a decade. The two-story Tudor home was still a bright blue with yellow and white trim. The picket fence around the backyard needed a paint job, but nothing major. The lawn was neatly mowed. The flowerbeds were in bloom. I walked to the front door and rang the bell.

When she answered the door, Janet's face registered shock, surprise, and disbelief in one expression, and that's not easy to do.

We stared at each other.

"Can I come in?" I said.

I sat in a chair at the island in the wide, bright kitchen while Janet poured coffee.

She must have just gotten off work at the hospital as she still wore her nurse's whites. Her sandy hair was in a ponytail. Her face had the creases and lines of a forty-six year-old woman, but they weren't unattractive. Just the opposite.

A few inches taller than Carol, Janet had the hips and figure of a woman who'd borne three children, but what fat there was on her was scarce. She watched her diet. Probably still jogged as she and Carol did together when Carol was still alive.

"I have to admit, John, you threw me for a loop," Janet said. "Showing up here like this."

"I should have called, but I didn't know what to expect," I said.

Janet took a chair opposite me at the island. "You mean I wouldn't have taken your call?"

"Something like that," I admitted. "Maybe."

"I would have," Janet said as she took a sip of coffee.

"And Clayton?" I said.

Janet sipped coffee, lowered the cup and smiled weakly. "Clayton ran off with the babysitter six years ago."

I stared at Janet. "Well, that threw you for a loop, didn't it?" she said.

"You're serious?"

"Mark was seven at the time," Janet said. "We had a regular sitter from the neighborhood. She was twenty-two. I wasn't. Boys will be boys. It didn't last. He wanted to come home. I wouldn't let him. A man hits you once; you don't go back for more, right?"

"Where's Mark now?" I said.

"Clayton's week to have him," Janet said. "We alternate weeks. He only got every other weekend in the divorce, but this way allows me to work full-time."

"The girls?"

"Clair is twenty-three and married," Janet said. "In five months, I'll be a grandmother. Julie is in her second year at Princeton. The tuition is a back breaker. She had better amount to something. She comes home when she can. Not often."

I sipped some coffee. "I missed a lot," I said.

We looked at each other.

Janet asked the question that begged to be asked. "Are you sober?"

"Almost five days now."

Janet sipped coffee. "Permanent?"

"I'd like to think so," I said.

Janet stood up and walked around the island to me. "Let me see your eyes."

"What?"

"Just look up."

I looked up.

Janet looked close.

"Okay," she said and went back to her seat.

"What were you checking for?" I said.

"Signs of liver damage."

"Find any?"

"No."

"The eyes are the window to the soul," I said.

"In more ways than one."

"Can I smoke?"

"As long as my son isn't home."

I pulled out my pack and lit one. Janet went to a kitchen drawer and returned with an ashtray.

"So, what's the real reason you're here?" Janet said. "I don't see or hear from you in almost a decade and you show up unannounced."

"Couple of reasons," I said. "One is to thank you."

"For?"

"Having the strength and presence of mind to sell the house, pay off my debts, and bank the rest for me," I said. "I'd forgotten all about it until recently."

"You're welcome," Janet said. "What's the

other reason?"

I drew in smoke, held it a moment, and exhaled slowly.

"Are you stalling?" Janet asked.

"Yes."

"Why?"

"I'm trying to remember if I've ever lied to you," I said.

"Have you?"

"I don't remember," I said.

"Are you going to lie to me now?"

"No."

"Want more coffee first?"

"Yes."

"Should I fix you something to eat?"

"I promised Oz I'd bring back pizza."

"Who's Oz?"

"He'll come up in the conversation," I said.

Janet went to the coffee maker on the counter and returned to the island. She filled both our cups, set the pot on a wood block, and sat.

"Go ahead," Janet said.

I started the story at the point where I awoke to a gloved fist in my face and took it all the way to needing pizzas for Oz. It needed twenty minutes and another cigarette. Janet watched me without expression. She didn't move except to sip from her cup.

85

I ended with, "So, here I am and that's why I'm sober five days."

"The man we believed was responsible for Carol's death hired you to find out who murdered her so he can die with a clear conscience?" Janet said. "You couldn't possibly make up that tale and expect me or anyone else to believe it, so it has to be true."

"I think what Crist really wants is to die knowing it wasn't his son," I said.

"Was it?"

"I don't know," I admitted. "Crist admitted his son was a hothead, but that doesn't mean he sent someone to murder Carol or to scare me off. Crist paid for a pocketful of judges, lawyers, and even jury members to make sure he and his family walked. His son had to know that."

"What if he didn't?" Janet said. "What if he did and didn't care or trust the payoffs?"

"That's possible."

I lit another cigarette.

Janet drank some coffee.

"What are you going to do about Regan?"

"Nothing for the moment."

Janet nodded.

"What's the other reason?" Janet said as she set her cup down.

"The question I couldn't face as a husband when Carol died," I said. "I have to ask as a cop, because I know the detectives working the case asked them while I was in the hospital."

"Question?"

"You're her sister and best friend," I said. "Could she have been having an affair with the man who murdered her? All good cops look at that angle in every domestic murder situation. I have to look at it now."

Janet quietly looked at me without emotion or expression. Equally as quiet, she stood up, walked around the island, and slapped me across the face.

Janet is a powerful woman.

The slap spun my head around and stung like hell.

Janet returned to her chair without saying a word.

I waited for my bell to stop ringing, then I stood up and said, "Well, I have some pizzas to pick up."

I started walking toward the front door.

"Jack?" Janet said.

For some reason, Janet always called me Jack, while Carol never called me anything but John.

I paused to turn around.

"Come to dinner next week," Janet said. "Mark would love to know he has an uncle."

"Sure."

"Wednesday is my half day at the hospital."

"I'll be here."

"Seven?"

"Sure."

I left and went to the Marquis. I didn't rub my cheek until I was behind the wheel. My sister-in-law packed quite a wallop.

11

Crist received me in the backyard of his mansion. We sat at the patio table under a retractable awning and sipped freshly squeezed lemonade in tall glasses filled with ice. The three acres of gardens were in full bloom. Campbell reclined topless beside the pool a quarter acre away from us. If she knew we were there, she didn't care enough to cover up or even acknowledge our presence.

I took a sip of lemonade and lit a cigarette.

"I'm not allowed alcohol," Crist explained when he sipped from his glass. "Do you know how boring life is without wine at the dinner table?"

"I'm learning," I said.

Crist chuckled. "I guess you are at that."

"Mr. Crist, do you have any idea how a police investigation works?" I said.

"I've been on the wrong end of them all my life," Crist said. "I know how to beat them, avoid them, and if all else fails, pay for them to go away."

I allowed myself a smile as I sipped lemonade. "In a case like this, where the evidence is nonexistent, the investigating officers squeeze the details for every drop until something falls out or it's a dead end. In a cold case, all there is to go on are the details and backtracking your footsteps."

"You're backtracking?" Crist said.

"And eliminating."

Crist nodded.

"I'd like to talk about your son," I said.

Crist nodded again. "I figured."

"You said he was a hothead," I said. "Capable of arranging for me to be scared off, as it were."

"Capable, yes. Guilty, that's why I hired you," Crist said. "Capable and guilty aren't the same thing. I'm capable of everything the papers write about me, but guilty of only half."

"In the case of your son, we don't know what the other half is guilty of," I said. "Isn't that why you hired me, to find out?"

"Yes."

"What was his relationship with you like?" I said.

"I'm not quite sure what you mean."

"Was he a good soldier? Did he question

your authority or follow orders without incident?"

"He did everything I told him to do," Crist said. "He didn't always like it and sometimes voiced his opinion, but he always followed my orders to the letter."

"What were his duties in the business?"

"As a kid or later?"

"When he died."

"Michael oversaw all my Vegas interests," Crist said. "The casinos, real estate, business investments, prostitution, and government."

"Government?"

"Who gets greased for a new zoning law or a liquor license, that kind of thing."

"Drugs?"

"No," Crist said. "Since the seventies, all my drug activities, including importing and sales, are contracted to middlemen. It costs a bundle to do business that way, but it can't be traced back to me because the middlemen don't know who employs them. No, Michael had nothing to do with my drug operations."

"What about money?"

"What about it?"

"Was he well paid?"

"He was my son," Crist said. "He was paid a handsome corporate salary from my business operations and a small fortune under the table as my captain in the field."

"So he had no need to secretly branch out for some extra income?"

"I would highly doubt that."

"How did he live?"

"If you mean above his head, no," Crist said. "He had the entire second floor of the mansion all to himself. He also had a small apartment in town, but it amounted to nothing. If he needed money it was because he was secretly funding NASA."

"Yet you feel he may have been involved with my wife's death," I said.

Crist looked at me.

"Because he was a hothead?" I said.

"Because there were bits and pieces I couldn't account for," Crist said. "Times when he was supposed to be in Vegas and wasn't. Times when he was supposed to be here and wasn't. Times when his own bodyguards didn't know where he was. The defense firm representing me thought his behavior suspicious and something the feds might focus on in court."

"You talked to Michael about it?"

Crist nodded. "So did the lawyers."

"And?"

"He said he had nothing to do with your wife."

"But he wouldn't account for his missing time?"

"No."

"Who benefited by killing him?"

"Nobody," Crist said.

"You said the Campo Family made a move in Vegas," I said. "They killed your son, you said."

"And I wiped out every member of the Campos in retaliation," Crist said as if ordering toast in a diner. "So nobody benefited."

"They had to know you'd do that when they killed Michael," I said.

"You would think so, wouldn't you," Crist said.

Stupid criminals. The cop's best friend, I thought. I said, "Do you still retain the same law firm for criminal matters?"

Crist nodded. "Lewis and Clark and Associates," he said. "A suite in the Monument Building. You want to talk to them?"

"Yes."

"I'll have Kagan set it up."

"Thank you," I said.

"I'm getting tired, Bekker," Crist said. "Are we done?"

"Almost."

I lit a fresh cigarette as I looked across the yard at Campbell. She had turned over to roast her back.

"What about Michael's friends and associates?" I said.

"He contracted out his own protection," Crist said. "His associates were my associates, here, Vegas, and everywhere else. His friends, I don't know. That was his business."

"Girlfriends?"

"I haven't a clue," Crist said. "You don't ask a forty year-old man who he's fucking. Whoever his women were, he kept them off the grounds."

"The apartment in town?" I said.

"And Vegas. For all I know, he could have a litter of kids somewhere."

"Can I get a list of his and your associates from that time frame?" I said. "My wife's death to your son's."

"I'll see Lewis and Clark have that ready for you."

"I'd like to see them as soon as possible."

"You have a number they can call you at?" Crist said.

I gave him my new cell number.

Crist looked past me at his daughter. Campbell was sitting up now, rubbing lotion on her naked breasts. "Have you visited your daughter yet?"

"No."

"Don't wait too long," Crist said.

12

I was home in time for lunch.

Along the way, I stopped at a pet store and purchased two bowls, a bag of dry food, a few cans of the wet stuff, a litter box, and a bag of litter. At a local sub shop, I picked up a meatball hero and a liter bottle of Coke.

I set the food and water bowl beside the card table and the litter box on the side of the trailer. I'd see how things went and if she took to them, I'd move them inside. She took to the food and water immediately. The litter box not so much. Why confine yourself to a small, plastic box when you had miles of beach?

I read a newspaper while I ate the sub. When I was finished, the cat surprised me by jumping onto my lap. I scratched her behind the ears.

"If you're going to live with me, you need a name," I said.

She purred.

"You look like a Molly," I said.

She purred some more. I took that as approval.

"Molly it is," I said.

Off in the distance, I kept an eye on the man walking along the beach. He was too far away to make out details, except that he wore a suit and carried a bag under one arm.

Molly rubbed her head against my stomach.

"Settle down," I told her.

The man was walking away from the shoreline and toward my trailer. A bit closer, I could see the man was a good size and walked with a familiar gait.

"Molly, I'll be back in a minute," I said.

I stood up, left Molly on my chair, and entered the trailer. I emerged ten minutes later with a pot of coffee and two mugs.

Molly hadn't moved from the chair, but she was sitting up, watching the man.

"John Bekker, you son of a bitch!" Walter Grimes shouted to me from a distance of a hundred feet.

I stood beside Molly and grinned. "I figured you wouldn't call," I said.

Walt arrived, set the bag on the card table, and extended his right hand. We shook, then hugged, then broke apart and grinned like a pair of idiots.

"Val said you sounded real good on the phone. I figured I'd stop by instead of calling and see for myself," Walt said.

Broad-shouldered with a barrel chest, the years had been kind to Walt. Except for a slight receding of the hairline, he appeared almost exactly as he had twelve years ago. He looked at Molly. "What's this?" Walt said.

"She just sort of showed up," I said.

"You fed her?"

"I did."

"She's yours."

"What's in the bag?"

"A little something from Pat's Donut Shop."

"I was hoping that's what it was," I said.

Pat's, a family-owned donut shop near my old station house, served a donut twice the size of Double D and heavier than Krispy Kreme. I hadn't had one in more than ten years. I realized I missed them. A lot.

"Pull up a chair," I said and filled two mugs with coffee.

Walt opened the bag. Six donuts the size of a catcher's mitt. Two Boston creams, two lemon creams, two double chocolate.

I snared a Boston cream.

Walt went for a double chocolate.

We dunked and bit off mouthfuls.

"I have to admit," Walt said, swallowing donut. "I didn't know what to expect when you called. It's been what, five years since we've seen each other?"

"At least," I said.

I chomped off more donut.

So did Walt.

"When did you make Lieutenant?"

"Four years and a few months ago."

"In for the full thirty, then?"

"I'll go until they force me out," Walt said. "Jonas lasted until he turned sixty-three. I think I can make that."

"Another fourteen or fifteen years?"

"I have nothing else to do," Walt said. "Worthwhile, that is."

I polished off the Boston cream and reached for the lemon.

"You know it should have been you with the bars," Walt said. "If things had turned out differently. Hell, you'd probably be captain and I'd have to shine your shoes every morning."

I bit into the lemon cream and sipped coffee to wash it down.

Walt lowered his donut and looked at me. "Hell, John, I don't know what to say here," he admitted.

I waved my free hand. "Nothing to say at this point. It's all been said."

"I guess."

"I've been sober for six days," I said. "Do you want to know why?"

"We got four more donuts to eat," Walt said.

"I'd like to save two for Oz."

"Who?"

"He'll come up in the conversation."

Two donuts remained in the bag by the time I ended my story. What remained of the pot of coffee was in our mugs. I smoked a cigarette and looked at Walt.

Walt's expression was somewhere between incredulous and stunned. "Holy mother-fucking shit," he said.

That probably was an understatement.

"You have a dead pool on Crist at the station?" I said.

"I don't indulge in such vulgar activities as to bet on a man's death," Walt said.

"He tells me four months tops, as early as three," I said.

"Well, I'll have to change my wager," Walt said. "I had him for six months on a ten spot."

"Walt, what can you do to help me out with this?" I said.

"You're not seriously considering this

lunatic's offer?" Walt said.

I looked at Walt.

"Oh, for God's sake, John."

"Like you said, I've nothing better to do."

Walt sighed. "I'll do what I can on the quiet," he said. "No publicity of any kind. One peep and the door's closed. And no more free donuts."

"I don't plan on opening it," I said. "And there's no such thing as a free donut."

"So what do you want?" Walt said. "And please make it something that doesn't cost me my pension."

"For starters," I said.

Walt groaned. "For starters generally means give me an arm and I'll take a leg."

"I'd like to talk with Stiles and Peterson and read their reports," I said.

Walt looked at me.

"What?"

"Dave Peterson is dead, John," Walt said. "Four years now. He was serving a warrant on a suspect deemed nonviolent. Dave knocked and the nonviolent suspect fired six shots through the apartment door, hitting Dave twice in the neck and the two uniforms with him in the arm and elbow. The nonviolent suspect was tripping on the latest designer drug and thought Dave was the repo man there to take away his fifty-seven inch TV."

"Jesus," I said. "He was married with kids, wasn't he?"

"Three girls. All teenagers."

"Stiles?"

"Pulled the pin two years ago," Walt said. "Twenty-three was enough."

"Know where he is?"

"Bought a bed and breakfast on the Cape," Walt said. "Runs it with his wife."

"Can I see the reports?"

"At the station," Walt said. "Read only. No copies."

"Viceroy?"

"The old ME retired five years ago. I got a number for him."

"Captain Jonas?"

"Retired a colonel. Passed away two years ago from a stroke."

"Matt Henin?"

"Took a promotion to the feds a few years back. I got a number for him, too."

"What's his name, the FBI agent who headed up the investigation?"

"You mean Paul Lawrence?"

"Right. And him?"

"Polishes a chair in Washington."

"The city or the state?"

"DC bound all the way."

"Got a number for him?"

"No."

"I'll find him," I said.

Walt sighed openly. "John, not that I want to talk you out of this, but have you thought it all through? What you're doing. Crist is a fucking savage, a real animal. You don't get to the top of the mob food chain otherwise."

"Did I leave out the part where he paid for Regan's private hospital for the last ten years?" I said.

"No."

I heard a nibbling noise and was pleased to see Molly at the food bowl, happily crunching on the dry food I left her.

"The thing is, John," Walt said. "Do you really want to dredge up all those memories and hurt? I mean . . . you're sober right now. One push and you're right back where you were a week ago. And besides, what can you do that the FBI and the entire department working round the clock for months couldn't?"

"Probably nothing," I said. "But, the reason I am sober right now is because of Crist, so I feel I owe it to him to at least follow through on this."

Walt's eyes shifted to Molly, who was giving herself an after-dinner bath by licking her paw and rubbing it across her face. He shifted his eyes back to me. "What do you want to do first?"

"Read Stiles and Peterson's reports," I said.

"Computer only," Walt said. "No hard copies, no notes."

"Tomorrow?"

"Yeah, yeah."

"Nine okay?"

"For Christ's sake, John," Walt said. He took a deep breath and let it out slowly. "Yeah, fine. But, listen, you freaking Viking, if you manage to stumble upon something the department doesn't know, you give it over immediately or no more . . ."

"Free donuts. Yeah, I know."

Walt looked around for a moment. "So how's the sunsets from this dump?"

"Stick around and find out."

"No thanks," Walt said, and stood up. "Some of us have a real job."

"Hey, Walt?"

"Yeah?"

"Thanks."

"For better or worse, we're still partners," Walt said. "Even if it's spiritual."

I nodded. "Yeah."

As Walt walked back to town, Molly jumped onto my lap, where she continued her bath. I scratched her behind the ears.

"So, do you come here often?" I said.

Molly ignored me and kept licking her paw.

"Yeah, that line never did work for me," I said.

"Best damn donuts I ever had," Oz said as we watched the Yankees trounce a miserable Kansas City team on ESPN.

Oz was taking the last bite of the second donut.

Molly was asleep on my lap, curled up in a ball.

Oz looked at Molly as the last scrap of donut disappeared. "You keeping her?"

"More like she's keeping me," I said.

"That's how it is with women," Oz said. "You chase them and chase them until they finally catch you. You think you run the show, but you don't. They just let you think you do."

Molly turned over and gave me her belly to rub.

Who was I to argue?

13

Valery Greene-Herman came out from behind the precinct desk to give me a hug and a kiss on the cheek.

"Lou told me you were coming," Valery said.

Lou being Walt. Lou being the common name for every lieutenant in every police station in the country.

I still didn't remember Valery. What had I done to make so lasting an impression on Sergeant Greene-Herman?

Valery looked at the shopping bag in my right hand.

"What's this?" she said.

"Take two, but keep it quiet," I said.

Valery looked into the shopping bag. "Pat's?"

I'd stopped by Pat's for three dozen of her finest. At three bucks apiece, they cost twice as much as twelve years ago. But, you can't put a price on a Picasso, or a great donut.

"Yum, yum," Valery said as she snared two.

"Walt in?" I said.

"And waiting. Second door on the . . . oh, hell, you know where it is."

By the time I reached the stairs, Valery had dug into her first donut.

The second floor is reserved for the precinct detectives, the lieutenant, captain, and two interrogation rooms. The holding cell is on the first floor behind a steel door painted to resemble wood.

The squad room is the first door on the right at the top of the landing. It houses twelve desks, one for each man or woman in the squad. Four detectives are assigned to Homicide, four for Vice and four for Special Crimes, an umbrella term for everything else. Homicide is the glory detail, but if your record is good enough in Special Crimes, you could make the Special Crimes task force in the DA's office.

I know that firsthand.

Adjacent to the squad room is the lieutenant's office. In this case, Walt.

Down the hall and isolated is the captain's office.

I knocked on Walt's door and opened it without bothering to wait for a response. The office hadn't changed much in twelve years. Same green metal desk against the window. Same flooring, walls, ceiling fixtures, file cabinets. The only change was the flat screen computer on the desk.

Walt was on the phone, his swivel chair turned to look out the window. "For Christ's sake, Bev," he ranted. "I need the manpower reports, maintenance budget, crime stats, and gangbanger activity reports on my desk two days before the captain returns from vacation." He paused to listen. "Thank you," he said, lowered the phone and turned to greet me.

He eyed the shopping bag. "Is that what I think it is?"

"What do you think it is?" I said.

"One of two things," Walt said. "The first is a bomb. Since I'm doing you the favor of your life, I see no reason for you to blow me up. The second, more probable, is a bag of goodies from Pat's."

"Three dozen goodies, minus the two for Valery on the way in."

"That's two dozen for the squad room," Walt said. "Those pigs will inhale them and beg for more. Two for me, two for you, and six for Venus Jackson-Brown as payment."

"Who is Venus . . . what?"

"Jackson-Brown, and she's the records officer around here," Walt said. "Payment for her off-the-books time is six donuts or one hundred and twenty-eight dollars per hour."

"I'll go with the six donuts."

"I thought you would."

"And that buys me what?"

"From now until lunch," Walt said. "That's the best I can do."

"Venus her real name?"

"Ask her. I've got to go to a meeting with some stupid community outreach crap."

"My mother named me for the goddess of love," Venus Jackson-Brown said when I asked her the question.

"Because she loved you?" I said.

"Because my father wasn't her husband," Venus said. "I was a love child."

"I brought you donuts," I said.

"Pat's?"

"Of course."

"Sit."

Venus tapped the empty chair next to her at the long desk. I set the donut bag on the small desk against the wall and sat.

Venus, a stunning black woman of about forty-five, showed me her smile. It was wide and bright. She had Eartha Kitt eyes, gray. Her hair was pulled back in a ponytail. Her uniform fit very nicely. A Smith & Wesson .40 sat holstered on her right hip.

"Seven-thirty this morning, Walt tells me to pull up everything on an unsolved murder case from twelve years ago," Venus said.

The first two buttons of her uniform were undone and her cleavage was busting a gut to free itself.

"He said a retired detective was stopping by to take a look," Venus continued. "I read them and called Walt to ask him who was coming by to read them. He said the victim's husband. That's you?"

"That's me," I said.

"I have no idea what to say," Venus said. She sighed and the third button of her uniform all but flew off.

"Say you'll show me the reports," I said.

Venus nodded and tapped on her keyboard. "What do you want to see first?"

"Anything by Art Stiles."

Venus clicked her mouse.

A page appeared on the flat screen.

"I'll get us some coffee to go along with my bribe," Venus said.

By the time Venus returned with two deli containers of coffee, I had read through all of Art Stiles' reports. It must have been difficult for a good detective like Stiles to admit after months of hard work that the investigation was dead. He marked it OPEN and put it on the back burner for a later date that never arrived.

"I'll allow myself one, but I'll eat two," Venus said as we dug into the shopping bag.

"Stiles was a good detective," I said. "He did everything he could to catch a break."

"But he didn't?"

"No."

"You want to see Peterson?"

"Yes."

We ate our donuts and drank our coffee while we read through Peterson's reports. Most of them were a repeat or duplicate of what Styles had to say, a hope and a prayer that the investigation would lead them somewhere close to a suspect or a scrap of hard evidence.

As I read the final page of Peterson's reports, I felt a brush against my left knee. Venus needed to adjust her legs after sitting for an hour, I figured.

"You want to take a break or continue?" Venus said after I read the final page.

"Walt put me on the clock," I said. "I have to clear out by noon."

"Who do you want next?"

"Let me see Matt Henin, then we'll close out with Viceroy."

Venus nodded and worked her keyboard, brushing her knee against my thigh in the process. This time, the contact lasted a bit longer before we separated.

I closed my eyes for a second, opened them, and looked at Henin's initial reports. The man and his CSI crew went through my house with a fine-toothed comb, gathering evidence and clues. There were plenty of hair fibers to analyze. Unfortunately, they belonged to Carol, our kids, and me. There was blood, mostly Carol's, a splattering of mine from my razor. No fingerprints from the intruder. No semen, blood, saliva, or anything else to say he was there.

Except his handiwork.

Viceroy's reports were brutal to read.

His findings indicated that Carol died hard, fighting to her last breath. She had multiple fractures and bruises on her face where the intruder beat her with his fists. She had severe bruises in the abdomen, indicating she took some hard punches.

I didn't know that.

Ultimately, Carol died from a crushed windpipe. From the purple discolorations, Viceroy put together a diagram of the intruder's hands. Viceroy estimated the intruder had size sixteen fists, nearly two inches larger than heavyweight champion Muhammad Ali in his prime and four inches larger than Lennox Lewis, a great champion from a decade ago.

The intruder was a big fellow. I knew that, but not how large a man he was.

Viceroy stated in his report that Carol's vagina was torn to shreds. The violence of his attack had to have been terrorizing for Carol and for Regan to witness. Viceroy stated that fluids from the attacker weren't present, indicating the attacker didn't ejaculate. Back to the "he used an object" theory.

Why use an object when you have a perfectly good penis?

Maybe the attacker was impotent?

Maybe he surprised Carol believing it was me and the attack got out of hand. Once Carol was dead, he used an object to make it appear like a rape.

My daughter had to see that.

Twelve years, she hasn't spoken a word.

Was it any wonder?

"I can't read any more of this," Venus suddenly said.

I looked at her.

"It's different when you know the people involved," Venus explained. "When there's a face to the names, it's no longer just stats and words. It becomes up close and personal."

"I understand," I said. "I'm done, anyway."

"Good," Venus said and moused off the page.

I stood up and arched my back.

"Want to talk about it?" Venus said.

"No."

"Got thirty minutes before I have to kick you out," Venus said.

"How long have you been in communications?" I said.

Venus grinned. "What you mean is, have I ever been a real cop. Rode a cruiser and walked a beat like a man?"

"Not what I meant," I said.

"Maybe not directly," Venus said. She shrugged her wide shoulders. "I'm a three striker. It makes you sensitive to questions."

"Three striker?"

"I'm a woman, a mother, and I'm black," Venus said. "Not the best recipe for advancement in police work."

"I don't believe that."

"Eleven years," Venus said. "Since my husband ran off with my best friend and I needed a stable schedule to raise my kids."

"I'm sorry to hear that," I said.

Venus grinned, then allowed herself a tiny laugh. "My best friend's name was Peter and he was gay."

"No shit?" I said.

"Married eleven years doesn't mean you

know a damn thing."

"No, it doesn't."

"What's your question after how long I've been in communications?"

"Notice anything in common about the reports?" I said.

"Besides the meticulous documentation and brutality of the words?"

I nodded.

"Two experienced detectives and one experienced CSI supervisor all failed to mention the possibility the victim might have known her attacker," Venus said. "They failed to check the possibility your wife was having an affair with her attacker, or if they did, they excluded it from their reports."

"Why?"

"They wanted to spare your feelings until it was absolutely necessary," Venus said. "Since they never had a strong lead or suspect, there was no reason to mention it. Or . . . they're not as good as you thought they were?"

"Not exploring that possibility means the man who murdered my wife got off the hook because they wanted to spare my feelings," I said. "That's really shitty police work."

"I agree," Venus said. "If it upsets you to think that, go with the stupid theory."

I grinned and looked at Venus. "When all else fails, go with stupid," I said.

"I've been hitting on you, you know," Venus said.

"I figured."

"Given what I've just read, I feel I should apologize."

"No need," I said.

"You want copies?" Venus said.

"Walt said I couldn't have them."

"We won't tell Walt," Venus said.

Venus made copies. I folded the sheets of paper and stuck them into my jacket pocket.

"So what now?" Venus said.

"I go home and think some more."

"I was thinking more along the lines of the sexual tension between us," Venus said.

"That what now."

"I figured."

"You figure a lot, but do you ever do anything about it?"

"I've been drunk an entire decade and sober a whole week," I said. "Putting my male ego aside a minute, a woman like you would finish me off right now. It would be disastrous for us and embarrassing for me. Truth is, right now I just don't have the strength to go toe-to-toe with you."

"Wow," Venus said. "That must have hurt to say."

"Not as much as not saying it," I said.

"I'll let it go for now," Venus said. "But, don't be surprised if I show up at your doorstep with a bag from Pat's one afternoon."

Walt was on his way in when I was on the way out. We stopped to chat on the precinct steps.

"How was your meeting?" I said.

"Morons still believe you can convert hardcore gangbangers with a group hug and a vegetable garden. We need fewer trees and more cops. How'd it go with Venus? Learn anything new?"

"Just that Stiles and Peterson may have tried to spare my feelings."

"Who didn't? Venus make copies for you?"

"Don't hold it against her," I said. "I wore her down with my charm."

"I expected no less."

"Just so you know, I plan to talk with Henin, Viceroy, and maybe Paul Lawrence," I said.

"I'd be surprised if you didn't."

"Who's captain of this dump now?"

"Stanley Weight transferred over from the six seven after Jonas pulled his pin," Walt said. "He'll last another eighteen months and then it's my turn, maybe."

"Need a written reference?" I said.

"Wise ass," Walt said. "Don't get too wise and cut me out of what you're doing. I want to know every move you make when you make it."

"Sure."

"I mean it, asshole."

"I know you do," I said. "Right now I'm going home to take a nap."

"I'm going to do the same, only from my desk with my feet up at the taxpayers' expense," Walt said.

"I'll call you later with an update," I said.

"Make it sooner than later," Walt said.

We parted ways.

I went home, made lunch and shared some of it with Molly.

14

There's a lot to be said for a really good sandwich. Same for a rusty lawn chair on the beach, a sunny afternoon, high tide, and thoughts to occupy your mind.

In the case of the sandwich, it was smoked, peppered turkey on a whole-wheat club roll, with a side order of thick fries and a quart bottle of ginger ale. Pat's donuts, no matter how heavenly, only went so far in appeasing the appetite.

In the case of high tide, dozens of surfers were riding the waves or splashing about, resembling seals from a distance. They were fun to watch and cheap entertainment.

As for occupying my thoughts, I read, then read again the photocopied reports that Venus supplied me from our meeting.

I learned nothing new.

Stiles and Peterson investigated much as I would have had Carol been a stranger and I drew the case. I questioned if I would have documented investigating an affair of the victim if I knew or worked with the victim's husband.

I decided that I would.

It didn't make me feel better or worse about Art or Peterson. It was just something I would do.

I called Art Stiles on my new cell phone after the sandwich. A woman who didn't identify herself answered and told me Stiles was out making a supply run. I left her the cell number.

Next, I dialed the number for Viceroy. A polite synthetic voice told me that the number was no longer in service. No longer possessing the authority to delve any deeper into that, I made a note to ask Walt to find out why.

Matt Henin answered his phone after two rings, but that was because Walt gave me his private number at the FBI lab in DC. After twenty years with CSI, Henin did the smart thing and moved to a federal position where he could work another ten and go out with an inflated pension for his lifelong commitment at studying evidence that would make a billy goat puke.

Henin was stunned into silence for a moment. Then he said, "Son of a bitch, John Bekker."

"Hey, Matt," I said. "How's the feds?"

"Pays a hell of a lot better than city work," Henin said.

"So does JCPenney."

"Now that I'm over my shock, how are you, John?"

"I'm not drinking after a decade of a nightly bottle."

"I don't know what to say to that."

"Say yes."

"To?"

"I'd like to fly out there and talk a few things over," I said. "I was thinking the next day or two."

"About Carol?"

"Yes."

"Just tell me when so I'm not out of the office."

"I'll give you a heads up tomorrow," I said.

"Look forward to it, John."

We hung up. I called Paul Lawrence. He didn't answer his own phone. I navigated through a mouse maze of press 1 for this and press 2 for that until I finally spoke to a living human being. In my case, a female with a no-nonsense attitude and approach to her job.

"Your call is being monitored and subject to trace," she said.

"I'm on a cell phone," I said.

"Not as difficult as you would believe," she said. "What's the nature of your call with Special Agent Lawrence?"

"We worked together on a task force assignment into organized crime some years back," I said. "I'll be in DC on business and thought I'd stop by and say hello."

"If he's available, please hold," she said.

Before I could inquire as to what happens if he's not available, music came on the line. I smoked a cigarette, listened to Kenny G, some John Tesh until, fifteen minutes later, Paul Lawrence ended the New-Age music festival by speaking.

"Detective John Bekker," Lawrence said. "This really you?"

"The John Bekker part, anyway," I said.

"You get the press 1, press 2, what the hell do you want routine?" Lawrence said.

"Followed by some Kenny G."

"God."

"I know it's short notice, especially given the fact we haven't spoken in a decade, but I'll be in DC on business in a few days and would like to stop by," I said.

"I'll get you a visitor's pass and we'll grab some lunch at the Hill Steakhouse," Lawrence said. "We might get to make fun of some congressmen and senators and the like."

"Sounds like a good time," I said. "I'll call you when I get in."

I severed the call and lit another cigarette. In the distance, dozens of black wetsuits bobbed like so many apples in the waves. Molly suddenly appeared at my side and jumped onto my lap. I stroked her back.

My cell phone rang. I picked it up and pressed talk.

A female voice said it was the office of Lewis and Clark and Associates calling, would I be available to speak with Mr. Clark.

I told her yes.

A short hold and Clark came on the line.

"Mr. Bekker, David Clark, representing Mr. Crist," Clark said in a professional voice. I had the feeling he rehearsed that voice in front of a mirror. "My understanding is that you're working for Mr. Crist and would like a meeting with my firm."

"Yes," I said as I stroked Molly. "Have you any details?"

"I spoke with Mr. Crist and Frank Kagan at length," Clark said. "When would you like to meet?"

"Tomorrow at nine okay?"

"Fine. See you then, Mr. Bekker."

I pushed the end button on the phone, then punched in the number for Walt.

"I'm not disturbing your nap?" I said when Walt picked up.

"Gotta work off those donuts somehow," Walt said.

"Just keeping you in the loop and up to snuff and any other cliché that fits I can think of," I said.

"Whose loop and what snuff?" Walt said.

I filled Walt in on my conversations with Henin and Lawrence and requested a number search for Viceroy. I told him I missed Stiles, but would catch up with him later.

"I'll run down Viceroy's number and call you back," Walt said. "When are you going to DC?"

"Tomorrow if I can swing it," I said. "No later than the day after."

"I'll call you later," Walt said.

"I'll be here later," I said.

I hung up, pocketed the phone, and carried Molly back to the trailer. I left her fresh food and water, locked my door, and pulled out the keys for the Marquis.

15

After an hour and forty-five minute drive to the Cape, I arrived at the bed and breakfast Art Stiles purchased after his retirement. It was an impressive-looking, three-story gambrel style building, with a massive front and back garden and a swimming pool/hot tub thing on the side. The solarium that faced the pool housed the breakfast nook. A paved parking lot had spaces for twenty cars.

I counted eleven. I parked and made it twelve.

I entered through the front door lobby. Nobody was there to greet me. Like most B&B's, after breakfast you're on your own. I wandered a few rooms, the sitting room, entertainment room, library, and breakfast nook. Furnishings were bright and cheery, with plenty of flowers and plants.

In the nook, I spotted Art Stiles through the glass. He was digging holes in the garden with a shovel to plant the new flowers that were in tiny boxes at his feet.

I opened the door and stepped outside.

Art paused and looked at me. At first, there was no recognition on his face. Then it hit him and his entire face lit up into a smile.

"John Bekker," Art said as he tossed the shovel and walked to me.

I held out my right hand. "Art."

"Monica said you called," Art said. "She wrote the number on a slip of paper and misplaced it in the kitchen. How the hell are you?"

"Sober."

Art shook his head. "That's good, that's good."

"Been a long time," I said.

"Years and years."

"How's Monica?" I said.

"Had what they call a mini-stroke a few years back," Art said. "She's fine except she's becoming more forgetful every day. Like with your number. Hell, she'll outlive the both of us, that woman."

"So she's okay, then?"

"Fine."

I nodded. "Can we go inside and talk?"

"Sure," Art said. "Want some coffee?"

"Love some."

■ ■ ■ ■

The coffee Art served was expensive gourmet, a dark and flavorful roast that topped anything I've had in recent memory. We chatted first before I stated the reason for my visit. Besides the mini-stroke, Monica survived several bouts with cancer early in their marriage. I didn't know that. At the moment, she was cancer free and except for slight forgetfulness, doing fine.

"When we were on the job, how come you never mentioned her cancer?" I asked.

"Monica, she likes to keep things close to the vest," Art said. "Even family didn't know."

Then I told Art about Crist and the purpose for my visit.

We sipped gourmet coffee and looked at each other as I filled Art in, each of us smoking cigarettes.

"Jesus Christ, Eddie Crist," Art said when I finished. "I figured that old bastard would live to see a hundred."

"The other reason I'm here, old friendships notwithstanding, is to ask some questions about Carol," I said.

"God, it's so long ago," Art said. "I probably remember half what you read in my reports."

"It's what's not in your reports I want to talk about," I said.

"I don't . . . what do you mean?"

Art's eyes had a slight, sudden hint of panic in them.

"If it was my case and there were no suspects and the woman was married, I would look into the possibility of a jealous lover," I said.

Art stared at me.

Art sighed at me.

Art said to me, "It wasn't pertinent to the case, John."

"What wasn't?"

"Aw, Christ," Art said.

"Tell me, Art," I said. "I need to know."

"Remember when you were studying for the sergeant's exam?" Art said. "Working forty-five hours a week and studying another thirty on top of that. She . . . Carol had what you call an office fling. She was alone a lot, John. I'm not saying she was right, but I can understand it. Some clown at work pays you a lot of attention, things just go too far. We checked the guy out. He was living in Seattle at the time of the . . . Carol's death. There was no reason to bring up dirty laundry that had no bearing on the case."

I stared at Art. "And you found out how?"

"Jesus, John."

"How?"

"Women keep secrets," Art said. "They're not like us. They don't wear their lies on their sleeves the way we do. Women hide things way better than we do. Even Monica. After twenty-six years of marriage, she's got a boatload of shit I don't know about and probably don't want to."

"That doesn't tell me anything," I said.

"Remember that big walk-in closet you had in your bedroom?"

"Carol's?"

"We found some letters in a shoebox," Art said. "Must have been forty boxes of shoes and one of them had these letters. Carol broke off the affair with him. She wrote she loves her husband and she came to her senses and she didn't want to do anything to jeopardize her marriage. We know that from his letters back to her."

I nodded. "The letters?"

"We . . . Dave and I, the captain, we all agreed to burn them."

"Walt?"

Art nodded.

"What else?"

"That's it."

"Your eyes tell me different."

"In the last letter she wrote, she must have . . . he wrote back asking for a . . ." Art paused, stubbed out his smoke, and lit a fresh one. "There is a slight possibility Regan might be his."

"Thank you, Art," I said.

Art looked at me.

I stood up and left.

I drove thirty minutes the wrong way on the expressway before I pulled over into the breakdown lane. I turned the engine off and sat in silence.

I beat the steering wheel and dashboard with my fists.

"Son of a bitch . . . cocksucker, motherfucker!" I screamed to no one.

I started to cry as I continued to pound the steering wheel.

Then I opened the door and leaned out to puke.

After that, I started the engine and drove home.

16

After a sleepless night of tossing and turning, I arrived at the station house around eight in the morning. I didn't bring donuts. I didn't stop at the desk where Valery Greene-Herman jumped to her feet as I raced up the stairs two at a time.

I didn't knock on Walt's door as I shoved it open and barged in.

Walt jumped to his feet. He started walking out from behind his desk and said, "Are you crazy?" I didn't hesitate for one second to punch him in the jaw.

The punch knocked Walt backwards, where he struck the wall

I came around the desk, shoving aside the chair.

Walt lunged off the wall and hit me in the waist like a tackling dummy. I struck a low filing cabinet next to the desk and fell backward to the floor.

"You stupid son of a bitch!" Walt shouted.

On my knees, I swept Walt's legs out from under him with my right arm. He went down next to me.

I jumped to my feet a second before Walt did and grabbed him in a headlock with my left arm.

"My neck, you stupid son of a bitch," Walt yelled, and then bit me in the left hand.

"No biting, asshole," I said as I punched Walt.

Walt stomped my right foot and I yelped.

"Ha!" Walt announced.

I was punching Walt in the face with my right fist when a dozen cops rushed in with weapons drawn.

Walt and I looked at the dozen pistols pointed at me.

"Are you people . . . Christ's sake, John, let me go," Walt said.

I released my hold.

Walt stood up. "What the fuck is wrong with you morons?" he said. "Put those guns away."

Valery holstered her weapon. "We heard the . . ."

"This is two old friends having a discussion," Walt snapped. "Get the hell out of my office and go fight some crime. Idiots."

They got the hell out.

Walt looked at me. "What the fuck was

that about?"

I picked up a fallen chair, righted it in front of the desk, and sat. "I'm not leaving until you answer a question."

Walt went and sat behind the desk.

I lit a cigarette.

"You can't smoke in here," Walt said.

"I can't punch a cop in here, either."

Walt rubbed his jaw. "What's your question?"

"Why did you leave my wife's affair out of the investigation?" I said.

"Fucking Art," Walt said.

"Never mind fucking Art and tell me," I said.

Walt quit rubbing his jaw and rubbed his neck. "They checked it out thoroughly," he said. "It had no bearing on the investigation. Not her murder or the task force. What was the point of dragging a six-year-old affair into the mix? You were close to the edge of a near breakdown as it was. We felt that would have pushed you to no return."

"Who was the man?"

"Christ's sake, John," Walt said. "What difference does that make now?"

"There's a chance Regan may be his."

"So what?" Walt said. "You're going to abandon her now? Look, you meathead, in case you haven't figured it out, Carol's affair was because she was lonely. It happens when young married women are left by themselves seven nights a week for months on end. Some moron at the office pays attention to them because their husbands don't. That's all there is to it."

"Where do I find this attention giver?" I said.

"He didn't kill Carol," Walt said.

"But is he the father of Regan?" I said.

"If you want to see that guy, look in the mirror next time you shave," Walt said. "Now get the fuck out of my office before I have you arrested for striking an officer."

"What happened to two old friends?" I said.

"Out!" Walt commanded.

I stood and walked to the door.

"Asshole," Walt muttered under his breath.

"From you that's a compliment," I said and slammed the door behind me.

I went down the stairs to the lobby and out to the street.

Valery grinned at me as I passed by the desk.

17

The office of Lewis and Clark and Associates was about what I expected. A big money firm with plenty of mahogany furniture, leather chairs and sofas, rows and rows of law books, and citations on the walls.

I met with David Clark alone in a massive conference room because, as Clark put it, "Mr. Lewis sadly passed away less than a year ago."

We sat at a highly polished mahogany table for twenty in leather chairs and looked at each other from opposite sides.

A pitcher of water and two glasses rested between us.

A stack of file folders and a legal pad was to Clark's left.

"Where shall we begin?" Clark said in his practiced, lawyer voice.

"I'll tell you what I want and you tell me if it's in that stack of papers."

"Fair enough."

"You know I was part of the task force on organized crime and that we were closing in on Crist and his crime family?" I said.

"I have an entire file on you, Mr. Bekker," Clark said.

"Mr. Crist believes he would have beaten the task force in court," I said. "Do you agree?"

"Yes," Clark said. "For every charge, we had a counter. For every accusation, we had a denial. For every witness against, we had two for. We had a meticulously prepared defense to counter a sloppy prosecution."

"You had judges, witnesses, and jury members bought and paid for," I said.

"So I've heard," Clark said in his voice.

"Do you believe Crist or his son sent a man to scare me off the case, which resulted in the death of my wife?" I said.

"No."

"How can you be so sure?"

"For one thing, it would have shown a total lack of common sense on the part of Mr. Crist," Clark said. "And Mr. Crist was never one to act carelessly. The whole point of his defense was to look less guilty, not more guilty."

"And his son?"

"Now that's a different story," Clark said. "It's exactly the kind of stupid, careless, hothead move Michael would have made. Except that he didn't."

"Can you prove that?"

"Michael was in Vegas the night your wife was attacked," Clark said. "His bodyguards all gave statements to that effect. So did his bodyguards in New York. They took polygraph exams and passed."

"That doesn't mean he didn't make the arrangements."

"Michael also took a polygraph concerning the death of your wife and passed," Clark said. "The tests were requested by me and conducted in this very room by a paid specialist the police often use. Shortly after that, the case against Mr. Crist fell apart and the federal prosecutors had no choice but to suspend their investigation."

"Did Michael ever pass a polygraph concerning the witness who was killed before he could testify against Crist in court?" I said.

"It never came up for reasons I just cited," Clark said.

"You're a very good defense lawyer," I said.

"I do what I can."

"I'd like to read those files."

"It's why I have them. You can make notes, but no copies. Would you like lunch while you read?"

"I would."

"What would you like?"

I hacked away at the files for three hours before the lunch I ordered arrived. I put away the medium rare steak, baked potato, carrots, and lemon-flavored water while I hacked away some more.

I read each page of each file carefully to the last word.

I made pages of notes.

I learned nothing.

Not entirely true. I learned that if ever necessary, I could never afford the fees charged by Lewis and Clark and Associates, even if Lewis was dead.

Mostly what I did was make lists on the legal pad.

Lists of defense witnesses, testimony, names, dates, times, and places. Lists of Motions of Discovery, where I read reports written by me that I'd forgotten about going as far back as thirteen years ago.

Lists of lists, none of which told me a damn thing.

Around four-thirty, Clark returned. The woman from the reception desk came in with him, carrying a pot of coffee, cream, and two mugs on a silver tray. She set the tray on the table and left without saying a word.

Clark poured coffee into each mug and splashed in cream.

"Figured you could use some about now," Clark said.

"Thanks." I took a sip.

Clark sat. "Learn anything useful?"

"I learned a great deal, just none of it useful to my cause."

Clark sipped from his mug. So did I. The coffee was excellent, though a step below what Stiles served in his B&B.

"Maybe not," Clark said.

"How so?"

"It is my understanding that Mr. Crist wants to die knowing that his son had nothing to do with your wife's death," Clark said. "Isn't that true in reverse?"

"By not finding any guilt, I prove him innocent?" I said.

"That is true, isn't it?"

"Only in court."

"Isn't that where it counts?"

"Not if you're Crist," I said.

"Or you?" Clark said. "Aren't you and Mr. Crist basically after the same thing, the man who murdered your wife?"

"We are," I said. "Can you help us?"

"I've held nothing back," Clark said. "Not

one scrap of paper."

"I'm not talking about paper," I said. "I'm talking about your impressions, gut feelings, and instinct as a lifelong defense attorney."

"You want to know what I think?"

"Yes."

"I think every one of the names in these files is a criminal," Clark said and tapped the files with his hand. "Some worse than others, but every one of them lacks compunction and all should be in prison. That's what I think. Does that help you?"

"No."

"What will?"

"Finding who murdered my wife."

"You think it's in here?" Clark said and tapped the files again.

"Yes."

"You think somebody paid to have you scared off the case," Clark said. "You weren't home, but your wife and daughter were and they paid the price."

"Yes."

"Do you believe Michael Crist is the man responsible?"

"Yes."

"The evidence suggests otherwise."

"It's more like the lack of evidence," I suggested.

"You were an excellent detective, Mr.

Bekker," Clark said. "Would you arrest a suspect based upon lack of evidence?"

"No."

18

Oz tossed fresh coals into the grill pit, doused them with lighter fluid, replaced the grill, and tossed in a lit match. A high flame erupted. It burned for a few seconds, then settled down to start graying the coals.

Oz turned to me. "Should be about twenty minutes."

I stroked Molly on my lap and nodded.

Oz took his chair next to mine.

We watched the coals start to ashen.

Oz opened a beer. He wasn't drinking the hard stuff. Was he cutting back on his alcohol consumption or unable to buy a bottle until the next check arrived? I didn't ask.

"I need a favor," I said.

"Sure."

"I'm going to Washington for overnight tomorrow," I said. "Can you leave her fresh food and water a few times a day?"

"The kitty cat?"

"Molly."

"No problem," Oz said. He sipped beer. "This about your daughter?"

"Yes."

"You visit her yet?"

"No."

"Well, when you're ready."

I nodded and stroked Molly.

"Man coming," Oz said.

I looked down the beach.

"That's Lieutenant Walter Grimes," I said.

"Cop?"

"The best. My former partner."

"Want I should get extra burgers and dogs?"

"He might be a bit mad at me," I said.

"What for?"

"I sort of punched him in the jaw this morning."

" 'Sort of'? How's that work, sort of?"

"Ask him when he gets here."

I lit a cigarette and smoked it to the filter. By the time I tossed the butt into the grill, Walt had arrived.

"Look at this bruise you gave me," Walt said as a greeting. "Not to mention a stiff neck, you fucking idiot."

"Oz wants to know if you're staying for dinner," I said.

"Got burgers, dogs, baked beans, cornbread, and chocolate ice cream," Oz said.

Walt looked at Oz.

"Sunset's real pretty this time a year," Oz said.

"Let me call Elizabeth," Walt said.

"Sure," I said.

Walt pulled his cell phone and called his wife. He spoke for a few minutes, then put the phone away and looked at me. "Liz said when am I bringing you home for dinner?"

"Is she still the cook I remember?" I said.

"Worse," Walt said. "Twenty-two years of marriage, the woman can burn spaghetti in a boiling pot."

"Tell her soon," I said.

"I'll get an extra chair for the lieutenant," Oz said.

Walt took the extra lawn chair and drank a beer. Oz did the honors at the grill. A bit later, the four of us, if you counted Molly as an us, ate from paper plates and watched the sun slowly sink into the ocean.

"Ever find who blew up the safe house and killed the witness?" I said, biting into a burger.

"FBI handled that one and the answer is no," Walt said.

"How's that possible, Walt?" I said. "How do you blow up a house, murder a witness and a half dozen FBI agents, murder my

144

wife, and leave not a single trace of yourself behind?"

"Money," Walt said. "Buys the best talent in the world. My guess is Michael Crist shelled out a small fortune arranging that one."

"The evidence and the Crist law firm say otherwise," I said.

"The evidence can kiss my ass in Macy's window," Walt said. "And so can Crist's law firm."

We ate for a while without talking and watched the glowing orange ball sink lower into the ocean.

"The percentage of unsolved crimes in this country is staggering," Walt said to break the silence. "Mind-blowing how many get away with rape, robbery, and murder."

"Are you saying my wife's murder is unsolvable?" I said.

"I'm saying you might have to live with that," Walt said.

I nodded.

Walt nodded.

Oz said, "Who wants ice cream?"

"What the hell," Walt said. "My cholesterol is too high to count, anyway."

The sun disappeared and replaced itself with darkness.

We ate ice cream and listened to the tide

145

roll in against the rocks.

"Sometimes, you just got to swallow hard and turn the page," Walt said.

I had no answer for that.

19

I caught a red-eye business flight that set me down in Dulles at eight-forty. As it usually is, Dulles was a packed madhouse of travelers.

Carrying a small gym bag of stuff, I skipped baggage claim and used my cell phone at the cabstand. I left a message for Matt Henin that I would be at his building within the hour.

Then I waited my turn for a cab.

Matt Henin worked out of a federal building in walking distance of Congress. He hadn't changed much since I last saw him more than a decade ago. About five eight, a hundred and seventy pounds, Henin had a slightly receding hairline as the only mark of time on him. Otherwise, he was still a baby-faced kid, even if he was pushing fifty.

We met in the lobby.

"You want a tour, or do you want to find a bench in the shade at the mall and grab some coffee?" Henin said as we shook hands.

"Bench," I said.

"You look terrific," Henin said as we walked outside to the street.

"And you still look twelve," I said.

We walked to the mall and found a vendor that sold coffee, selected a bench in the shade, and sat.

I opened the gym bag and removed the Pat's bag. "Got a couple for each of us," I said.

"Only thing I miss about back home," Henin said as he sucked up a Boston cream.

I took a double chocolate.

We ate our donuts and sipped our coffee.

"So what brings you to the capital of the world, as they who live here refer to it?" Henin said.

I told him.

Henin said, "Holy shit. Crist, huh."

"I read all your reports, yours and your staff," I said. "They didn't help much."

"Nothing helped much," Henin said. "I'm sorry we didn't do better for your family." He nibbled on the Boston cream. "And you," he added.

"Any theories?" I said.

"On?"

"How a man can break into my home,

148

rape and murder my wife, and then up and vanish like a fart in a twister," I said. "Like he didn't exist at all."

"Nothing I could document," Henin said. "Nothing I could testify to in court."

"We're not in court," I pointed out. "We're on a bench drinking coffee and eating three-dollar donuts."

"Theory?"

I nodded as I nibbled on my double chocolate.

"Somebody paid somebody else to scare you off the case," Henin said. "That somebody was to subdue you and threaten your family while you sat by helpless and watched. You weren't home. He didn't know that. He decided to deliver the message through your wife. Things got out of hand. He faked a rape afterward to make it appear that was the intent."

"That's about how everybody involved sees it," I said. "Question is, how does the attacker vanish like he did without a trace left behind to tag him?"

"I didn't see it much on the local level, but with the feds it's a common occurrence," Henin said. "But, it's not so difficult to grasp. You kill the hired killer to remove the evidence and witness."

I nodded. "Who? How?"

Henin shrugged. "Find who and you got the how and the man behind it all."

"Michael Crist and his entire crew passed poly exams," I said.

"Anybody pathological could pass them," Henin said. "Or take a certain type of blood pressure medication one hour before the test is administered."

"Propranolol," I said.

"Would be my first choice."

I nodded. "Back at CSI, how many rapes did you see where objects were used on the victim?"

"You really want to talk about this?" Henin said.

I nodded.

"Maybe three dozen in twenty years," Henin said.

"So it's not frequent, but not uncommon," I said.

"Rape is a crime of violence," Henin said. "In some cases, the rapist is fueled by so much hate, he uses an object afterward to mutilate his victim."

"Ever have one where just an object was used?" I said. "The rapist never penetrated the victim for whatever reason."

Henin thought for a moment. "No."

"I wonder if there's any stats on that," I said.

Henin shrugged. "Give me your number."

I walked around a bit and took in some sights. I stood before the White House and Capitol building, Congress and the Lincoln Memorial, and ended at the Vietnam Wall.

Mostly I sat on a bench, drank coffee, smoked cigarettes, and killed time with my thoughts.

I was pissing on my own leg and pretending it was rain.

That's how much I had to go on. That's how far I'd progressed.

Not very far.

I met Paul Lawrence in front of the federal building the FBI calls home. He appeared a bit thinner and a lot more tired than I remembered. He had thick, wavy hair the color of wheat when we worked together. It was now thin and mostly gray.

Twelve years will do that to you.

That and chasing terrorists.

We shook hands.

Lawrence had a firm, quick handshake.

"Good to see you again, John."

"You, too."

"It's hot," Lawrence said. "Let's grab a steak. I'll show you how the government really works."

We walked the half-mile to the Hill Steakhouse. By the time we reached the massive, air-conditioned restaurant, my shirt was stuck to my back and my suit jacket stuck to my shirt.

Five minutes in the cold air took care of that.

The steakhouse was packed. Lawrence made a reservation for two and we took in the festivities while we waited for our meals to arrive.

Congressmen made deals with senators, lobbyists made deals with White House staff, reporters made deals with everyone, and everybody ate steak in air conditioning.

"I never got the chance to tell you how sorry I am about your wife," Lawrence said as we sipped iced tea.

"Thank you," I said.

"Your daughter?"

"In a medical facility where they treat trauma," I said. "Going on twelve years now she hasn't spoken a word."

"I'm sorry, John," Lawrence said. "I really am."

"Off the record, I'd like to ask you some questions," I said.

"Off the record, I'll give you some answers," Lawrence said.

"The bomb that killed the witness and your men," I said. "What was it?"

"C-4 with a mercury switch on a timer," Lawrence said. "A real pro job. It didn't come cheap, that's for sure."

"Any suspects?"

"Not many hit men for hire use C-4 or even know how to use it," Lawrence said. "Old time IRA, maybe. Terrorists with the right training. Russian mafia with connections. Ex-military gone rogue. Mercenaries. The thing is, despite TV and movies, C-4 doesn't grow on trees. Somebody really knew what they were doing and had access to the right tools."

"Money talks," I said.

"Enough of it does."

"So a pro takes out the witness," I said. "Same pro with the hit on me?"

"Too coincidental to be otherwise."

"Kill the witness, kill the cop with knowledge of the witness, wipe the slate clean, and nobody goes to court," I said.

Lawrence nodded slightly.

"Nobody except FBI knew the location of the witness," I said. "And the pro. Ever find the source of the leak?"

"No," Lawrence said. "Off the record, the Bureau reached the conclusion there wasn't a leak. Just sloppy police work."

"You mean the FBI was tailed, maybe bugged?" I said.

"That's what the report reads."

"You believe it?"

"No."

"What do you believe?"

"Off the record?"

I nodded.

"I think some son of a bitch sold out to Crist and set us up," Lawrence said.

"That would have cost a bundle."

"Crist has a bundle," Lawrence said. "Lots and lots of bundles."

"Any proof?"

"Not a shred."

"Hence the 'not a leak' report."

"Hence."

"Is the case still active?"

"Open, but inactive unless something pops."

"You checked financial records at the time?"

"Of everybody," Lawrence said. "No large transactions, cash transfers, deposits, nothing. Whoever arranged it paid in cash. Whoever pulled it off received in cash. Clean. Traceless. Professional."

"Only if you got millions inside a mattress," I said. "And don't believe in banks."

"Safe deposit box, perhaps?"

Our steaks arrived.

We ate slowly.

"How many qualified hit men haven't been seen or heard from in twelve years?" I said as I munched a piece of forty-eight dollar steak.

"The problem with that theory is that with the truly great ones, nobody has a file on them until they screw up and are finally caught or killed," Lawrence said. "A big time pro could operate for decades before anybody even knows he's alive."

"So who's been caught or killed in the past twelve years or so nobody ever heard of before?" I said.

Lawrence stared at me.

I ate another piece of steak.

"I'll find out," Lawrence said.

We finished off lunch with an eight dollar and fifty-cent hunk of chocolate cake rich enough to cause heart failure and five dollar a cup dark roast coffee. The bill came to one hundred and thirty-five dollars.

I left two hundred dollars of Crist's money and we walked back to the federal building even slower than we'd walked to the restaurant. Nothing like humidity-fueled heat and a full stomach to slow a body down.

"When you find out, give me a call," I said as we shook hands.

"Off the record," Lawrence said.

"Only way I work these days," I said.

Lawrence walked up the hundred or so steps and entered the building through massive revolving doors.

I sat on a bench inside the Mall and smoked a cigarette. I had reservations at the Mayflower Hotel nearby. I was tired and didn't want to get back on a plane. I could have used a long night's sleep.

I knew that wouldn't happen in a hotel room.

I grabbed a cab to the airport and caught the five-thirty business flight home.

Oz was in his usual spot in the lawn chair.

Molly was sleeping on mine.

She seemed genuinely happy to see me.

20

Walt and I were eating scrambled eggs with grilled English muffins in a diner one block away from the precinct.

"Elizabeth says I should bring you home," Walt said. "She said you could benefit from a home-cooked meal and a family type atmosphere."

"And you told her?"

"Whose cooking and what family?"

"You sleep on the sofa?"

"Not in my house," Walt said.

We ate some eggs and nibbled on muffins.

"I have two vacant bedrooms with the kids away at college."

I nodded as I sipped coffee.

"So this theory of yours, checking for dead hit men, there might be something to it," Walt said. "Some international pro, a ghost in the system, who knows? A name in Interpol, Scotland Yard, or the FBI database, he goes out of circulation never to be heard from again. It's a something."

"Or a nothing," I said.

"Yeah, but I like it," Walt said. "A mysterious international hit man is recruited to take care of the witness. Somebody unknown in America. He does the job and is rewarded for his troubles with a bullet in the brain and a swim in the river. It works. As far-fetched as it sounds, it works."

"So he what . . . blows up the witness and then takes a drive to my house and kills my wife before they clock him?" I said. "Or are there two separate contracts?"

"I don't know," Walt said. "But if you think about how much money, power, and contacts Crist has, he could pull something like that off."

"Except that Crist is the one who wants me to find who murdered my wife," I reminded Walt.

"Not Junior," Walt said. "Junior's dead, remember. Junior was a hothead. Remember? Junior may not have believed he could beat the case in court, or just plain didn't care and decided to buy himself some insurance. Junior was a psycho."

I looked at Walt.

Walt looked at me.

"You're a hell of a fucking cop, Bekker," Walt said.

"Want some more coffee?" I said.

"Yeah."

I waved our waitress to the table.

We sipped fresh brew and were silent for a moment.

"You won't do anything stupid," Walt said.

"Like drink a liter of scotch every night for ten years?" I said. "Like that?"

"I was thinking more along the lines of trying to work this alone," Walt said. "You could wind up as dead as Junior or a permanent missing persons report."

"I wouldn't worry," I said. "In all likelihood, Crist will die of his cancer before I make any real progress."

"Yeah?"

I sipped coffee. "Who gets the check?"

"You," Walt said. "Definitely you."

21

While Janet dipped chicken cutlets moistened with a milk and egg wash into Italian breadcrumbs in the kitchen, I tossed a baseball with her son Mark in the backyard.

He was twelve, but scrawny by today's standards. Today's twelve-year-old boys are the size of sixteen-year-olds in my day. Nonetheless, he possessed a decent arm and knew how to make a curve ball curve and a cutter cut across the plate.

"You ever play on a team?" Mark asked me as I tossed him a knuckleball.

"Once. A long time ago."

"Were you any good?"

"Couldn't hit the fast ball," I said. "Or a curve, a change up, sinker ball, or anything else they threw at me."

Mark paused to look at me. He nodded as if he understood my troubles, which he probably did, then went into his windup and tossed me a heater that was in the low sixties.

I held the ball and walked across the yard to Mark.

"You're releasing the ball too late," I said. "You won't get a good follow-through and you'll lose speed on your fastball. Even a two hundred hitter will tee off on that."

I held the ball, went into a windup, and stopped at the release point. "Here," I said. I followed through with my knuckles a few inches above the grass. "You end your follow-through as if you're reaching for something on the mound."

Mark nodded.

I tossed him the ball and walked across the yard. I squatted down and held my bare hands out to give Mark a target.

He took his windup and released the ball close to the point I showed him. The pitch was off target, but a good eight to ten miles an hour faster.

My hand stung. "Have another glove?"

"In the shed," Mark said. "It used to be my dad's."

I got the glove.

Mark threw twenty consecutive fastballs. Each had a little more pop than the previous. Some were even on target.

I stood up. "What we need to work on . . ."

"Is washing up for dinner!" Janet called from the open kitchen doors.

"But, Mom!" Mark said.

"No buts, young man," Janet said. "Just because school is out doesn't mean you get to do what you want. In. Wash."

Janet returned to the kitchen.

"Moms," Mark said.

"Can't live with them, can't live without them," I said.

"Tell me about it," Mark said.

We went in and took turns washing our hands at the kitchen sink.

We ate dinner at the butcher-block table on the far side of the large kitchen. A lamp hung suspended from the ceiling.

"Breakfast and lunch we eat at the chef's island," Janet explained. "Dinner is always at the table. House rule."

"Uncle Jack knows how to pitch," Mark said. "Can't hit a lick, though."

"Your Uncle Jack had a dozen college scouts drooling over his fastball, but he decided to enter the police academy instead," Janet said. "He was clocked at ninety-seven miles an hour when he was seventeen."

Mark gave me a flabbergasted look. "You became a cop instead of a pitcher?"

"Police officer," Janet said.

"Police officer," Mark said.

"I was a better cop . . . police officer than I was a pitcher," I said.

"With a ninety-seven mile an . . ." Mark said.

"Eat your dinner," Janet commanded her son.

We ate. The breaded chicken was crisp with a hint of Italian seasoning. The mashed potatoes and carrots were perfect. So were the biscuits. Mark drank chocolate milk. Janet and I settled for iced tea.

We talked baseball. Janet was a big fan, something Carol was not. We talked about Mark's grades. He was an A minus student, his lone B coming in math. He promised to do better next year. We talked about the hospital where Janet worked as a nurse. Mostly, we just talked the way families are supposed to but don't.

After dinner, before dessert, Mark and I rinsed and loaded dishes into the dishwasher.

"I didn't think cops did stuff like this," Mark remarked.

"We brush our teeth and make our beds, too," I said.

"Aw, geeze," Mark said.

Out of the corner of my eye, I caught Janet grinning.

"Who wants to help me eat this cake?" Janet asked as I was drying my hands.

Lemon with a cinnamon drizzle, we ate slices at the table. Mark licked icing off his fingers and before Janet could chastise him, I did the same.

Mark grinned in appreciation for saving his bacon.

After dessert, Janet sent Mark upstairs to his room to take a bath. "No arguments or the TV stays off."

Mark looked at me. "I have the official MLB game on the TV, Uncle Jack."

I looked at Janet.

"Bath first, then you can play, but just one game."

Mark flew up the stairs to his room.

"Want to take coffee outside?" Janet said.

I nodded.

We sat in recliners with the patio table between us, sipped our coffee, and looked at the blanket of stars above our heads.

"Should I ask?" Janet said.

"Ask, but I have nothing new to add to the other day," I said.

"But you won't give up?"

"No."

"Ever?"

I shrugged. "For a while, anyway."

Janet sipped coffee and thought for a moment. "Thank you for tonight. Mark needs a man in his life once in a while to do boy stuff with."

"His father?"

"Clayton is too interested in his latest conquest to pay much attention to him," Janet said. "And Mark has a hard time trying to figure out why his father hangs around with women young enough to be his babysitter."

I sipped coffee and looked at the stars.

"And frankly, so do I," Janet said.

"It's no secret, the male midlife crisis thing," I said. "We look in the mirror one day and see a stranger looking back. We buy sports cars and chase women half our age to recapture what we lost, or think we lost."

"You?"

"I drank through mine," I said. "So I basically missed it."

"What about now?"

"No sense having one now," I said. "I'll be ready for the rocking chair soon."

"I doubt that."

"You don't see what I feel," I said. "Which is about two hundred years old."

Janet sipped coffee and we were silent for a minute.

"Jack?" she said to break the silence. "You're not alone, you know."

"I know."

"No, I mean, you have me," Janet said. There was a long pause before she added, "If you want me."

It took a moment to sink in, then I turned my head to look at her. She kept her eyes straight ahead.

"Remember at your wedding, how I cried and cried?" Janet said. "I was crying because you married my sister instead of me."

I shifted my weight in the chair.

"Don't say anything," Janet said. "Not yet."

We sat for a moment.

Mark burst through the sliding doors, wearing pajamas and slippers.

"Game's all set, Uncle Jack," Mark announced.

Janet looked at me.

"Go on," she said.

I went inside. We played nine innings. Mark beat me three to two by scoring a run in the bottom of the ninth. He raced outside to tell Janet. I stood in the door to watch.

"I beat him, Mom," Mark said, excitedly. "I beat Uncle Jack."

"That's great, Mark," Janet said as she stood up. "But it's time to say goodnight."

"Aw, Mom."

"Your uncle has a very long drive home,

Mark," Janet said.

"Why can't he stay in the spare room?" Mark said.

Janet looked at me. "Maybe next time."

I said my goodnights to the boy at the base of the stairs. He gave me a hug. Janet watched from behind us.

Mark raced up the stairs.

I turned and looked at Janet.

"Well," I said. "I have a long drive."

"You do."

"I could . . ."

"Call first. My shifts at the hospital have a way of screwing things up."

I nodded.

Janet watched as I opened the door and went outside, got into the Marquis, and started my long drive home.

22

By the time I reached home, the sky had clouded up, blocking the stars and half moon. The beach was pitch-black. I could hear the waves crashing behind me, but could not see them as I left the Marquis and walked to the trailer.

I dug out my keys.

I caught a fleeting glimpse of shadow one second before a fist drove deep into my kidney.

I sank to one knee.

A kidney punch is one of the most painful and dangerous blows the body can endure. That's why it's illegal in boxing.

I needed time to recover from the punch.

My attackers knew that and didn't afford me any. Three men went to work on me, raining body blows, kicks to the ribs and face until finally they dragged me inside.

I woke up with my hands and feet tied with rope to one of my wooden kitchen chairs. I tasted my blood in my mouth. I couldn't see out of my left eye. It was swollen shut. The right eye wasn't much better.

I squinted to see.

Three men were ransacking the trailer.

One of the three noticed I was awake. He nudged the other two. They surrounded me. They were wearing black ski masks and leather gloves.

"What are you looking for?" I said.

Nobody answered.

One man reached for a paper bag on the table. He removed a liter bottle of scotch from the bag and twisted off the cap.

"It's not your brand," the man said. "But, hey, booze is booze, right, drunk."

The other two men grabbed my head and forced my neck back.

"Drink up, Mr. Bekker," the man with the bottle said.

The bottle was shoved into my mouth. Scotch filled my throat. It burned and I gagged. I spit some of it out, but the scotch kept coming. I swallowed in order not to choke on it.

"That's a good boy," the man said. "Drink or drown."

I drank.

My head went light.

The room started to spin.

I drank.

"Only half a bottle to go, Mr. Bekker," the man said.

The others laughed.

I could feel the alcohol build up in my blood. My brain and senses dulled. I was being poisoned by the very drink I'd used to get me through a decade.

I went under.

Somebody said, "Aw, look, he left some."

"He's done," somebody else said. "Let's go through this dump one more time and split."

I went down.

I thought I died.

It wasn't so bad.

A great deal like going to sleep.

23

I opened my eyes and peered through a veil of hazy white until slowly the fuzz cleared and I focused on the hospital bed I was presently occupying. Sheets covered me from the neck down. An IV tube was in my left arm. Monitoring devices were on my chest and right arm.

I shifted my eyes to the man asleep in the chair against the wall.

It was Oz.

A white bandage covered his forehead.

I shifted my eyes over to Walt, who was reading a newspaper in a chair against the wall. He lowered the paper and looked at me.

"It lives," Walt said.

"What . . . happened?" I rasped.

"That old man there saved your bacon," Walt said. "Took one in the head doing so, too. Seems three men jumped you, beat you, tied you to a chair, and shoved a liter of scotch down your throat. Oz heard something and came to check it out. He bumped into them when they were leaving. He had a hunk of driftwood and used it to fend them off, but three against one is never good odds."

"No," I said.

"Anyway, he comes to, goes inside, and calls 911," Walt said. "And here you are."

"John, you okay?" Oz said. "I heard you guys talking."

"I'm alive, thanks to you, Oz."

"Oz, the nurse wants to see you at the station down the hall," Walt said. "She wants to change that bandage."

"You want me to bring you anything?" Oz said to me.

"I don't think so, Oz," I said. "My stomach feels like it's lined with lead."

"Be right back," Oz said and left the room.

Walt stood up and went to the window to look out.

"I've been here how long?" I said.

"Thirteen hours," Walt said and turned around. "They pumped your stomach and treated you for alcohol poisoning and a concussion. Oz didn't show up, I'd be going to your wake instead of your hospital room."

I nodded.

"Oh, and you're pissing blood," Walt said.

"Right this second?" I said.

"Earlier," Walt said. "If you want an update, I'll call a nurse."

"No."

Walt sat in Oz's vacant chair.

"So tell me about it," Walt said.

"Apparently, you know more than I do," I said.

"My men tell me they tossed your place pretty good," Walt said. "What were they looking for?"

"I don't know," I said. "When I get home, I'll look around and see what's missing."

"Like they were after your treasure," Walt said.

"Possibly my notes," I said.

Walt nodded. "See if you found anything vital?"

We looked at each other.

"Have you?"

"Beats me," I said. "I took pages of notes, but if they add up to anything yet, I don't know about it."

"But somebody thinks you do," Walt said. "And they sent a trio of pros to put a stop to it, kill you, and remove what you know from the scene."

"I don't think they were there to kill me," I said. "They could have done that in the dark outside my trailer when they jumped me. I think they wanted to scare me off with a message."

"Go back to being a drunk and leave it alone?" Walt said.

I nodded.

Walt nodded.

"Who is behind the message?" Walt said.

I shrugged.

"You touched a nerve," Walt said. "Somebody knows you're poking around and that somebody is connected to twelve years ago."

"Seems that way," I said.

"Did they get your notes?"

"Ask Oz," I said.

Walking into the room wearing a fresh bandage, Oz looked at Walt.

"Ask me what?" Oz said.

"The men who attacked me and you, did they go near my car?" I said.

"Walked right by it on their way back to town," Oz said.

"You're sure?" Walt said.

"I made like I was out so they'd leave, but I wasn't," Oz said. "I stayed down until I knew they were far enough away not to see me get up."

"My notes are on the front seat," I said.

"I want to see those notes the minute you get out of here," Walt said.

"Where are my clothes?" I said.

"Whoa, wait a minute," Walt said. "You're not going anywhere until a doctor says you're ready to leave."

I sat up in bed. My head was spinning, but I tried my best not to show it.

"Want I should tie him down?" Oz said.

"No, get a nurse or a doctor for this fool," Walt said.

I sat with my legs over the edge of the bed. My feet didn't touch the floor. It was a very high bed.

A doctor checked my eyes with a tiny flashlight, put the light away, and frowned at me. "Mr. Bekker," he said. "You've had your stomach pumped less than thirteen hours ago. Not to mention the severe beating."

"I won't mention it, then," I said.

"This is not a laughing matter," the doctor said.

"Can you hold me if I want to check out?" I said.

"No, I can't," the doctor said. "But I won't be held responsible for what happens."

"You won't be."

"You'll need a nurse to check in with you from time to time for at least three days. I can arrange that for you."

"That won't be necessary, doctor. He's got one," Janet said from the corner of the room. "I'm a nurse."

24

When we arrived at the trailer, I spooned the beef broth with vegetables Janet prepared into my mouth, from a large soup bowl I didn't know I owned.

I don't like broth much.

I don't know anybody who does, really.

A greasy burger with fries would have suited me better, but I took Janet at her word that it would have made me very uncomfortable if not sick.

On my right, Oz dozed in a recliner, and why not? He was sleepy from the foot-long meatball sub he'd consumed while I was stuck with broth.

On my left, Molly slept curled in a ball on the card table.

Behind me, the door to the trailer was open. I could hear pots and pans rattling, and other such domestic noises.

The rattling stopped and Janet appeared with a glass of iced tea and took the lawn chair beside the card table.

"I like what you've done with the place, Jack," Janet said. "When was the last time you changed the sheets on the bed?"

"When did the Dodgers win the World Series last?" I said.

Janet rolled her eyes and sipped iced tea.

"And laundry?" she said.

"Let me think who was in the White House," I said.

"For God's sake," Janet said.

"How long do I have to eat broth?" I said.

"Later tonight, I'll fix some sandwiches," Janet said. "We'll see how you do."

"Coffee?"

Janet shook her head. "Too much acid for now. I picked up a six-pack of root beer. You can have that for the time being."

Oz groaned and woke up.

"My head feels like a high-pressure cooker about to blow," Oz said.

Janet stood up.

"Let me change your bandage and get you a pain pill," she said.

Janet entered the trailer and returned a moment later with clean bandages, a bottle of something, two root beers, and Oz's prescription from the hospital.

Janet gave me a root beer.

After removing the bandage from Oz's

head, Janet used the bottle of something to clean his cuts, then she redressed it with clean bandages. She opened the prescription bottle and gave Oz one pill and the root beer.

"Another in four hours," Janet said. "By then you should be in bed."

"Yes, ma'am," Oz said.

Janet looked at me.

I had a cigarette going while I drank the root beer.

"And you shouldn't be . . . oh, the hell with it," Janet said and took her chair. "Go on and smoke yourself to death."

Molly woke up briefly to look at Janet, decided nothing much required her attention, and returned to her nap.

"And where did this thing come from?" Janet said. "It looks like a stray."

"She," I said. "And I named her Molly. She wandered by one night and decided to stick around."

"Have you taken it to a vet for shots?" Janet said.

"No."

"I could use a shot," Oz said as he looked at his bottle of root beer.

"Go ahead," Janet said. "Have one. See what happens with that painkiller in you."

"Don't worry, Oz, she's bound to leave," I said.

"Don't bet on it," Janet said. "I shipped Mark off to Clayton for the week."

I sipped root beer and looked at Janet.

"I'm going to put a load in the washer," Janet said and stood up.

"I didn't know I had a washer," I said. I looked at Oz. "Did you?"

Oz thought that hilarious and started to giggle.

"How you feeling, Oz?" I said.

"Pretty damn good," Oz said, giggled, and closed his eyes.

Janet shook her head and entered the trailer.

Much to Molly's dismay, I gently moved her off my notebook where she was napping. I lit a fresh smoke and opened to the first page.

I read.

I saw nothing that would cause three men to work me over and pour a liter of scotch down my throat, then ransack the trailer.

My notes were questions without answers.

They didn't know that.

They believed I possessed something I didn't have.

Who are they? If you look deep enough, "they" usually becomes just one.

Who is the one?

The answer was in my notes.

Even if I didn't see it.

I thought about it.

I realized I possessed something valuable, which I had yet to figure out.

They didn't know that.

They were after my notes as verification. Roughing me up was a warning. Back off or worse was yet to come. Since they didn't find my notes, a second warning would surely follow.

Warnings are like that. A rattlesnake shows and shakes its tail. A cobra rises up and opens its veil. Some heed the warning. Some do not.

Twice in twelve years, a warning was on my head.

I heard a phone ring. I heard Janet speak in muffled tones, then she came outside with my cell phone.

"Matt Henin from Washington," Janet said.

I took the phone.

Janet stood in the background.

"Matt, how are you?" I said.

"I could use a few more Boston creams, but otherwise good," Henin said. "I've been tracking some numbers. Turns out there are a fairly high percentage of rapists who like to use objects. Everything from crucifixes to wine bottles and in between. However, the percentage of rapists who just used objects is less than one percent. Of that one percent, fifty percent are in prison for life, most going back fifteen years. The rest are on probation scattered throughout the country."

I lit a fresh cigarette.

"Anybody my way who was active twelve years ago?" I said.

"A handful," Henin said. "Want the names?"

I grabbed the pen next to Molly.

"Go ahead," I said.

Henin read me the names and I jotted them down, along with last known addresses. Five altogether. A very long shot, but a shot nonetheless.

"No need to tell you this is off the record and QT," Henin said.

"None," I said. "Watch your mail."

"For?"

"A gift."

I pressed end, tucked the phone into my shirt pocket, and looked at the names.

A real long shot.

Janet sat in the lawn chair. "That was about Carol, wasn't it?"

"Yes."

"Should I not ask questions?"

"I have no answers," I said. "Not yet."

"The men who jumped you, they'll return, won't they?"

"Probably," I said. "Once they realize I've ignored their warning."

"Why not listen?" Janet said. "Why go on with this? To please some old gangster because he's dying?"

"Because Carol's death needs closure," I said. "I owe her that much."

"My sister's been gone for twelve years," Janet said. "I've put her to rest. Why can't you?"

"Carol isn't just gone," I said. "She didn't pack a bag and hop on the bus, Gus. She was brutally raped and murdered and the man who did that to her is still out there walking around. I've stirred the pot and he's noticed. Good. Let him come to me again. Next time they won't find it so easy."

"To do what?" Janet said. "Get yourself killed?"

I lit a cigarette and stared off at the beach for a moment.

"It's too late," I said. "I pushed the rock down the mountain and it's gaining momentum. I can't stop it now, even if I wanted."

Janet's eyes appeared to water. She stood up and entered the trailer without saying a word. The door closed.

Oz opened his eyes.

"You're one smooth talker, Bekker," Oz said. "Like rubbing sandpaper on a balloon."

I sucked in smoke and held it for a moment. I exhaled through my nose and reached for my root beer.

"The woman's smitten with you and you act like she wasn't even there," Oz said. "Maybe you were a great cop once, but you got the common sense of a stray dog chasing its own tail."

"I'm a target now, Oz," I said. "I'd rather not have anybody in the bull's-eye on my back until this is over."

Oz sat up, then stood up. "And when will that be," he said.

Oz turned and started walking to his trailer. "I think I'm going to sleep in my bed for a while," he said.

I watched Oz walk to his trailer and enter it. He came to my aid and possibly saved my life, but he was a civilian and didn't grasp the criminal mentality. For men like Eddie Crist, his son, Michael, and the man responsible for Carol's murder, the rules were whatever they wrote for themselves.

It's like that with most criminals. From a purse snatcher to a mass murderer, the rules are their own. The line they crossed is the one they drew.

If they returned and Janet was with me, would they kill me and let her go?

I think not.

Same for Oz.

By the time civilians understood those rules, it was generally too late.

Janet was washing dishes at my tiny sink when I entered the trailer.

"I don't think it's safe for you to stay here right now," I said.

Janet froze at the sink.

"Do you want me to go home?" she said without turning around.

"It occurs to me that whoever is behind what happened the other night may have me under surveillance," I said. "I think it's too late for you to go home."

Janet turned around. "What are you saying?"

"Try to . . . for Christ's sake, can we make some coffee?"

"I think it's okay now."

Janet filled the coffee maker and as it dripped, I sat at the table to light a smoke. By the time the cigarette was finished, Janet set two mugs on the table.

She sat opposite me.

"Try to what?" Janet said.

"Understand," I said and lit a fresh smoke.

"If they can't get to me, they could use you to get to me. Worse. Mark."

"They would do that even though we have nothing to do with this?"

"They wouldn't hesitate one second."

Janet sipped her coffee. "What are you suggesting?"

"Listen and don't argue," I said.

I dug out my phone and dialed Walt's number.

He was still at the office.

"I need a place to stash Janet and her son," I told Walt.

There was a short pause, followed by a deep breath. "Yeah, I can see that."

"Got anyplace?"

"City has a house not far from the river they use for short term witness protection," Walt said. "It will be a tough sell to the DA to let us use it without an active investigation, though."

"I'll pay for it and some extra pay detail for police protection," I said. "But they have to be from your house. Nobody outside."

"How soon?"

"Tomorrow," I said. "As early as possible."

"I'll be in the office at eight," Walt said. "What about tonight?"

"I'm good."

"You sure?"

"No, but it's too late to worry about it."

"Nothing like confidence," Walt said. "Call me at eight."

I lowered the phone and looked at Janet. "Any questions?"

Janet slowly shook her head no.

"What did you pack and bring here?" I said.

"Enough for a week."

"That will do for now," I said.

"I'm going to clean and scrub what passes for the bathtub," Janet said. "Then I'm going to soak until my skin resembles a prune."

I nodded.

Janet got up and entered the bedroom. I waited until I heard water running, then I went over to the oven and slid out the bottom drawer where I kept pots and pans. From behind the Bundt cake pan I've never used, I removed the hard plastic gun case I placed there years ago.

I brought the case and a full mug of coffee outside to my chair.

Molly was awake and at her food bowl beside the open door.

I set the mug and case on the card table. I opened the gun case and looked at the Browning Hi-Power 9mm pistol. It was perfection in gun making. Blued with custom rubber grips and adjustable sights, the pistol held thirteen rounds in a clip and one in the pike.

I removed it from the case.

It was perfectly balanced in my right hand.

An old friend, saying hello.

I removed the clip and the round from the chamber, then broke the gun down to its basic parts and wiped them all with a rag. I went back inside and dug out the gym bag I stashed under the sink and returned to the lawn chair.

From inside the gym bag, I removed a cleaning kit, two fifty-round boxes of 9mm ammunition, a switchblade knife, a retractable baton, and four extra clips for the Browning.

From a side pouch, I removed a pair of thick leather shooting gloves I'd never worn while firing a weapon.

I oiled the Browning and reassembled it, then loaded the four extra clips.

The sun was going down.

I stuck the Browning in my belt, packed up the gym bag and case, and went inside.

Molly meowed at the door.

I let her in and locked the deadbolt.

25

Janet came out of the bathroom wearing a white robe over pajamas and gym socks. Her hair was still wet and slicked back. She wore no makeup, or none that I could detect.

Honestly, she didn't need any.

She filled a mug with coffee and joined me on the sofa.

"What now?" Janet said.

"We stay here tonight and move you in the morning," I said.

"My son and his father?"

"It's doubtful they know I'm out of the hospital yet," I said. "They're safe, but I'll ask Walt if he can have a car swing by every few hours."

Janet nodded as she sipped coffee.

"Walt used to be your partner," she said. "I remember him from a few barbecues years ago."

"He's a good man and a good cop," I said. "The best."

Janet looked at Molly, who was curled up in a ball on the sofa between us. "As good a cop as you?"

"He made lieutenant," I said. "And I doubt Walt would have spent a decade inside a bottle had the situation been reversed."

"Don't forget that you're human. None of us are as weak or as strong as we think we are."

"Small comfort," I said.

Janet looked at the Browning stuck in my belt. "Would you use that?"

"Yes."

"I remember you shot three men in the line of duty," Janet said. "Two of them died. One was at my hospital. Remember?"

I nodded. "It's not something you forget."

"So how is this going to work?" Janet said. "You'll keep watch all night while I sleep?"

"The windows have hurricane shutters," I said. "Nobody's getting in that way. I'll stay on the sofa on the odd chance they know I'm home. If anybody's out there, I'll know. I'll call 911 and if I have to, I'll use this."

I patted the Browning.

"I'm afraid," Janet said.

"We're never as scared or as brave as we think we are," I said.

Janet grinned weakly. "Small comfort."

"This is just a precaution, that's all," I said.

"That's enough."

"So, any chance I can eat something now?"

"Twenty-one hours, I think so."

"Want to watch a baseball game?"

"Sure."

Turns out, Janet had loaded up on the groceries before picking me up at the hospital. She decided broiled chicken cutlets with green vegetables would suit my still delicate stomach.

We cooked. I set up TV trays and put on the game of the week. Seattle against Baltimore. Those of us without cable have to settle for what we can get for free.

By the fifth inning, dinner was consumed and we watched the remaining four innings over coffee and cinnamon crumb cake. The cake was store bought, but good nonetheless.

After stacking dishes in the sink, I announced I was off to take a shower.

"Can I keep the TV on?" Janet said. "For the noise."

"You can sing and dance if you want to," I said. "Nothing's going to happen tonight."

"And tomorrow?"

"You'll be in Walt's very capable hands," I said.

I showered long and hard, letting the hot water seep into my sore, aching muscles. There was a purple bruise on my kidney, but at least I wasn't passing blood. The hot shower helped, but not much. I dared not shave, fearing my cuts and bruises would open up again.

I came out of the bathroom wearing a towel around my waist.

Janet was in the bed, sheets up to her neck.

"Let me grab some clothes and I'll be out of your hair in a minute," I said.

"I'm not a girl, Jack," Janet said. "I haven't been one for twenty-five years."

"Yes," I said. "I know that."

"I want to make love, Jack," Janet said.

I stared at her.

"I don't think I can," I said.

"I understand, Jack," Janet said. "The years of drinking, the hospital, I understand. Performance anxiety."

Janet patted the bed.

"Come here."

I walked closer to the bed.

"Here."

Janet extended her hand to me, palm open.

I looked at the little blue pill.

"It's Viagra, Jack."

"I've never."

"I snuck a peek at your hospital chart," Janet said. "You have the vitals of a twenty-year-old. It's safe. No side effects. Well, except for the desired one."

Janet put the pill in my hand and reached for the root beer bottle on the nightstand. "Take it."

I put the pill in my mouth and washed it down with root beer.

"Now what?" I said.

"You've just activated the launch sequence," Janet said. She flipped off the covers to reveal her naked body. "Let's go to stage two."

I slipped on a pair of shorts and snuck into the tiny living room for a smoke. Janet was asleep under the covers, so I did my best not to disturb her.

I grabbed my pack, lit one, and sat on the sofa next to Molly. She looked up at me, decided I wasn't too interesting at the moment, and returned to napping.

I sat in silence and smoked. I grabbed a root beer from the fridge, sat, drank, and smoked another.

Janet came in wearing a long tee shirt.

"I didn't want to wake you," I said.

"You didn't."

Janet sat next to me, scooting Molly over a bit.

"You didn't cheat on Carol," Janet said. "She's been gone twelve years now. If she were alive, this never would have happened. But she's not alive and we are."

Janet was right, of course, but it was still a bit sticky making love to a woman who used to be my legal sister-in law and I guess still is.

I nodded.

"I would have sold my soul to the devil if I could have done this twenty years ago," Janet said. "But I couldn't. Not to my sister."

"Carol had an affair once," I said. "I only found out recently."

Janet nodded. "She told me. She said it was the worst mistake of her life. She made me swear never to mention it to anybody."

"The anybody meaning me," I said.

"It doesn't change anything that you didn't know," Janet said. "Or now that you do know."

"No, it doesn't."

"I don't feel guilty."

"I don't either," I said. "I have a question, though. It's been two hours, how long does it take for this to wear off."

"It's still . . . ?"

I nodded.

Janet took my shorts and pulled them down to my ankles. She sat on me and removed the tee shirt.

"No sense wasting it," she said.

Annoyed, Molly jumped off the sofa.

"That's one way to get this fur ball to move," Janet said.

26

Around six the next morning, I woke Oz from his Tylenol 3–induced sleep.

He wasn't happy.

"Dammit, man," Oz complained. "I was dreaming I married all three Supremes."

I handed him the mug of coffee I'd carried over. "They're older than you, Oz. What's wrong with Beyoncé or Lady Gaga?"

"Got no heart, these young girls," Oz said. "What's a Gaga?" He sat up in bed and took a sip from the mug. "Now that I'm awake, why?"

"Moving day," I said. "Be dressed, packed, and ready to roll by seven-thirty."

"Packed?"

"At least for a week."

Oz sat up in bed. "The lady nurse?"

"Her, too."

"Good," Oz said. "I'm low on these super pills."

At one minute past eight, I dialed Walt's private number. He answered before the second ring.

"I convinced the DA it was necessary to place your sister-in-law and her son into protective custody," Walt said. "You'll have to pay for the special duty detail, though. Six-man team, two on for eight hours. Forty-eight an hour."

"No problem," I said.

"Did you get six winning numbers?" Walt said.

"Better," I said. "I got Crist."

Janet was silent the entire drive to the station. She sat next to me and looked out her window, occasionally shifting her weight in the seat.

In back, Oz stroked Molly on his lap. At first, she didn't want to go, but once in she seemed to enjoy riding in a car.

Walt was standing in front of an unmarked cruiser when I pulled in alongside it and shut down the engine.

Walt leaned into my open window. "Oz, you and the lady transfer over to this car. Three officers will ride with you. Another three will ride ahead. John, I'll ride with you."

Ten minutes later, we moved out.

Walt handed me a container of coffee and held another for himself. "She doesn't look too pleased about this," he observed.

"Would you be?" I said. "Two days ago, she was raising her son in the suburbs where all she had to worry about was keeping the lawn mowed."

Walt nodded. "Understandable. The old man?"

"Precaution," I said.

"We'll swing by after we make the drop for her son," Walt said. "What about the boy's father?"

"I'll tell him to leave town for a while," I said.

"What if he won't go?"

"He'll go," I said.

Walt looked at me.

I lit a cigarette and turned left behind the second car. "Did I see Venus in the first car?"

"You did," Walt said. "At forty-eight bucks an hour, this is a plum assignment. I had everybody put their names in a box and drew six names and two alternates. Venus tossed her name in and got picked. I think she might be sweet on you, John."

"Sweet I don't need," I said. "A shotgun I need."

"I think your sister-in-law might be sweet

on you, too," Walt said.

"Can we forget the sweet and think about the job at hand," I said.

Walt grinned, nodded, and sipped coffee all at the same time.

"Jesus," I said.

A block from the river, down a long dirt road, stood the safe house. It was the sixth and last home in a large cul-de-sac that was beset on three sides by thick, inaccessible woodlands and marsh.

"What, no moat?" I said.

"Cutbacks," Walt said. "You know how it is."

"Yeah."

I parked behind the cruisers and stayed in the Marquis.

"Not going in?" Walt said.

"I'm going for the boy."

"Not without me you're not," Walt said. "You sit here until I get back."

Walt and the parade of officers led Janet and Oz into the safe house. As she neared the front door, Janet glanced back at me and I nodded to her.

Behind Janet, Venus glanced backward and gave me a nod of her own.

An officer opened the door and they filed into the safe house.

I lit a cigarette and waited for Walt.

I thought about my lie while I waited. I felt guilty as hell for sleeping with Janet, although I wasn't sure why. Carol had been gone a long time now and I knew she wouldn't want me to spend the rest of my life drunk and alone. But, would she approve of sex between her sister and her husband?

I lit another cigarette and continued to wait, occasionally sipping the now cold coffee. *All in the Family* was a great title for a sitcom, but I doubted it applied to my situation.

Finally, Walt and two officers came out and walked to the Marquis.

"Know where the boy is?" Walt said as he slid into the front passenger seat.

"Yes."

"Then let's get him."

Clayton lived about a mile west of Janet's home in a two-story townhouse on a quiet street. He was home when we arrived.

"Nice townhouse," Walt remarked. "What's he do, the boy's father?"

"Stress engineer," I said. "Owns his own business and hires out to construction companies for major projects. Bridges, tunnels, dams, that kind of stuff."

Maybe a year or two older than Janet, Clayton had that superior attitude people adopt when they believe they're the smartest person in the room. In Clayton's case, it applied only if he were alone.

To his credit, Clayton waited until Walt finished explaining the nature of our visit before he acted like an asshole.

"I have no problem with you taking the boy," Clayton said. "But I see no reason why I should vacate my home over some sordid police affair that doesn't concern me."

I looked at Walt.

"Where's the boy now?" Walt said.

"In his room," Clayton said. "I was measuring the stress of a bridge under construction in Brazil when you arrived. I don't allow him to play while I'm working."

Walt looked at me.

"Could you get the boy?" Walt asked Clayton.

Clayton went up the stairs and returned a minute later with Mark. The boy wore a loaded backpack. He seemed genuinely happy to see me.

"Uncle Jack!" Mark exclaimed. "I've been working on my follow-through like you showed me."

"We'll talk about that in the car," I said. "I need a minute alone with your father."

"John," Walt said to me.

"I'll be right out," I said.

Walt glared at me, then put his arm on Mark's shoulder and steered the boy to the front door. I waited until I heard the door close.

"Clayton, you were an asshole twenty years ago and nothing's changed," I said.

"Fuck you, Jack," Clayton said. "Now get out of here. I'm busy."

"Don't get the wrong idea," I said. "I don't give a shit about you, but Mark needs his father, as big a dick as you are, so if you won't listen, I'll just have to make you listen."

"You haven't the authority, Jack," Clayton said. "You're not a cop anymore. You're nothing but a drunk."

I pulled the leather shooting gloves from my suit pocket.

"You have until I put these gloves on to agree to leave for at least one week," I said.

Clayton looked at the gloves. "Or what?"

I slipped the left glove onto my left hand.

"I'll call my lawyer," Clayton said.

"You do that," I said.

The second glove was on my right hand.

Clayton looked at the statue on the end table beside the sofa. A heavy piece of African art. He grabbed it and held it like a club.

"I'll use this," Clayton said.

202

"You do that," I said.

Clayton raised the statue and I punched him in the stomach.

My right fist went deep into Clayton's gut and momentarily paralyzed him. The statue fell to his expensive rug, but didn't break. Then he fell to his knees and gasped for air like a clogged vacuum.

I took Clayton by the arms and lifted him onto the sofa. I shoved his head down between his knees.

"Breathe," I said. "You'll be fine in a minute."

Clayton sucked wind as he raised his head to look at me.

"I'll be back in two hours to check on you," I said. "If you're still here, I won't be so nice. Find a motel somewhere in the country. Enjoy the quiet. Don't come back for one week."

I returned to the Marquis and got behind the wheel.

Between the two officers in the backseat, Mark leaned forward.

"Why are you wearing gloves, Uncle Jack?" Mark said.

Walt looked at me.

"Yeah, Uncle Jack," Walt said. "Why are you wearing gloves?"

27

Doctor Richards approved my unannounced visit to the Crist mansion. Crist had been taking a nap when I arrived. I left the Browning in the glove compartment, anticipating a pat down that didn't come, then was ushered into the large study.

"I'll try to be brief, but I could probably use at least an hour," I told Richards.

Richards nodded and left me alone in the study. I killed time by reading book titles in the wall-to-wall bookcases. Crist was an avid reader of world history, judging by the titles.

I was skimming through one of the many bios on Lincoln when the study doors slid opened and Crist rolled in, accompanied by Richards.

I replaced the book and looked at Crist.

The man appeared thinner and weaker than a week ago.

"Don't look so horrified," Crist said. "I won't go tomorrow. My doctor here says at least a month, maybe six weeks."

"I have some news," I said. "It will take some explaining."

Crist turned to Richards. "I want to sit outside and get some fresh air."

Richards nodded.

"Have them bring out whatever you say I can drink," Crist said. "And make it cold."

Richards nodded a second time and left the study.

Crist looked at me.

"Get the doors," he said.

I got the doors.

Crist rolled outside and I closed the doors behind us. He stopped at the patio table under the shade of an extended awning.

Almost before I could sit, a wingtip arrived with a tray of lemonade and two glasses full of ice. He poured for both of us. Crist nodded to the wing tip and he went to the pool and took a seat where he could keep an eye on us, or me.

Crist took a sip from his glass, smacked his lips, and looked at me. "I have a climate controlled wine cellar with a half million in wines from around the world. I have a separate facility just for Italian liquors worth a quarter mil and here I sit with a five-cent glass of a kiddy drink."

I sipped my lemonade. "They say the best

things in life are free."

Crist looked at me and his lips formed a tiny grin. "You know who says that?" he said. "Poor people say that because they will never drop a thousand dollars on a red wine with dinner or buy a Rolex on a whim. They say that because they have no choice but to accept what's free because they'll never buy what's expensive."

Crist took another sip and set the glass on the table. "What's your news?"

"Can I smoke?" I said. "I think better when I smoke."

Crist nodded.

I lit up.

I required forty-seven minutes and thirty-one seconds to detail my recent events. Crist drank his lemonade while he listened. I paused to refill both glasses and he drank half of his before I was done.

"I knew I was right hiring you," Crist said. "You got to somebody fast. That somebody is responsible, directly or indirectly, for your wife's murder."

"Probably true," I agreed. "But I have no idea at this point if your son was involved or not."

Crist stroked his bony chin while he thought. "Your face. They worked you over pretty good before they filled you with booze."

"They knew what they were doing," I said. "Likely pros for hire instead of in-house flunkies."

"You can tell that from a beating?"

"The way they knew how to ambush me," I said. "Exactly where to hit me to disable me quickly, the way they searched my house. No wasting time or movements. When my neighbor surprised them, they didn't kill him because there was no need to. They were pros and damn good ones at that."

Crist nodded.

"The boy and his mother, they'll be safe with the police," Crist said. "I'll pick up the tab for their protection."

"Should I tell them that?"

Crist grinned at my suggestion. "That the crime boss they've been after for thirty years is paying the overtime for the cops?" he said. "I doubt the prick DA has much of a sense of humor."

"I could use a good shotgun," I said. "Something semi auto, no pumps, double barrel or breech loaders."

Crist looked past me at Wing Tips.

Wing Tips stood up and walked to the table.

"Bekker needs a shot gun," Crist said. "Semi auto, nothing pump."

Wing Tips nodded to me and said, "I'll have it for you when you leave," turned and entered the mansion through the study.

"Okay?" Crist said.

"Sure."

"Now one last thing, Bekker," Crist said. "You have my word your daughter's medical bills will be paid until the day she passes. I want your word that if I go before you've cleared my son's memory, you will continue on until you do or you prove him guilty. Either way."

"You have my word," I said.

Crist nodded. "Who said cops and criminals can't exist side by side?" he said softly, with a slight grin.

I stood up from the patio table. "Should I get somebody to help you back inside?"

"No," Crist said. "I want to enjoy the fresh air for a while."

"I'll be in touch soon," I said.

Wing Tips met me in the living room with a large steel case in his right hand.

"This should do nicely," Wing Tips said.

I took the case.

"Call it a gift," Wing Tips said. "We have a dozen more nobody uses. The good old days are gone."

28

I brewed some coffee and sat with a mug at the card table, smoked a cigarette, and looked at the steel gun case.

As gun cases go, it was a nice one.

Waves from the tide rolling in crashed against the rocks, creating mild thunder. Gulls battled for scraps in the sand. A slight salt sea breeze blew across my face. An altogether pleasant afternoon.

I crushed out the butt and opened the two hasps on the case.

I lifted the lid and looked at the M-4 shotgun. Black, with a pistol grip, the M-4 was the choice of the U.S. Marine Corps. I hefted the shotgun, held it by the pistol grip, and peered down the sights. Loaded, the magazine held four plus one in the pike. At two grand from the factory without options, modifications or scopes, it was the best shotgun money could buy. So said the Marine Corps.

Two boxes of 12-gauge ammunition and a cleaning kit were included.

I removed five shells and loaded the magazine.

I drank some more coffee, smoked another cigarette, and thought for a bit.

My cell phone rang.

It was Paul Lawrence from Washington.

"Feel like dinner?" Lawrence said.

"When?"

"Tonight."

"I'll need to check flights."

"No need," Lawrence said. "I'll be there by seven."

"You're coming here?"

"What's the point of having a fleet of planes if you don't use them once in a while?"

"That's what I always say. Should I pick you up?"

"I made arrangements," Lawrence said. "Let's eat in, okay?"

"Sure."

"Later," Lawrence said and clicked off.

I set the cell phone on the card table and thought some more. Lawrence didn't want to talk on the phone. He didn't want to chance a leak or a tap into his or my phone. Tapping a cell phone is next to impossible unless you have the right equipment. The phone company and the feds had such equipment.

Lawrence had news meant for my ears only.

I packed the M-4 into the case, brought it into the trailer, and slid it under the bed. With the Browning in the small of my back, I entered the Marquis and drove to town.

The coals were white hot when I spotted a sedan making its way across the beach. I stood up and tossed two steaks onto the grill. They made that satisfying sizzle steaks make when the grill is at optimum temperature.

I sat in my chair and waited for the sedan to arrive.

Lawrence drove himself. He parked beside the Marquis, exited, and walked to me. I stood up and extended my right hand. We shook.

"Nothing smells like steaks on a hot grill," Lawrence said. "Smelled them as soon as I hit the beach."

"Want a beer?" I said. "I'm on the wagon, but I picked up some for you."

"I'll have one with dinner," Lawrence said. "Got any coffee?"

I brought a full pot and two mugs from the kitchen. We sat, sipped, and listened to

211

the waves crashing against the rocks.

There was no rushing an FBI agent, especially one with news.

"His name was Fagan Alowishus Cavanaugh," Lawrence said.

"An Italian guy, huh," I said.

Lawrence grinned and sipped coffee.

I got up to turn the steaks. I used tongs rather than a fork. Nothing dries a steak out quicker than holes poked in it when on a hot grill.

"He was a British Marine back in the late sixties, turned IRA in the seventies," Lawrence said. "Claimed responsibility for six major bombings and a dozen other minor ones. Around eighty-seven or so, when the Brits made peace with the IRA, he left Ireland and went freelance."

I sipped coffee and lit a cigarette.

"Sold his talents to the highest bidders in Europe, Asia, and here in the States," Lawrence said. "Mob work, mostly."

"Oh?"

"I thought you'd like that," Lawrence said. "We got a file on him two inches thick, but what the CIA and Interpol have on him reads like *War and Peace.*"

I got up again to flip the steaks.

"In the early nineties, Cavanaugh did some major hits for the Vegas, Miami, and

New Orleans mob," Lawrence continued. "Took out an entire warehouse in Miami by the docks and two cat houses in Vegas that muscled in on Crist territory."

"So Crist knew him then," I said.

"That I can't confirm," Lawrence said. "Cavanaugh always worked through a middleman who made his arrangements and took payments. Knowing how Crist operates, there were probably a half dozen go-betweens who set things up for him. The CIA tracked six bank accounts in the Cayman Islands, Bahamas, and Aruba to Cavanaugh. Our office kept close tabs on those accounts with the idea in mind somebody would slip up and lead us to him."

"But nobody did."

"No."

"Still?"

"Well, here's where things get interesting," Lawrence said. "A week before the bomb killed your witness, one million U.S. was deposited into the Cayman Islands account."

I stared at Lawrence.

"The CIA and my office sat on it for weeks, then months, then years," Lawrence said. "That was the last deposit ever made. No withdrawals, transfers, or any movement of any kind. Finally, the CIA decided to move on his accounts to try to smoke him out, and nothing. A worldwide search produced nothing. He either retired or somebody decided he shouldn't come down for breakfast anymore."

"A hit on the hit man," I said. "Remove the witness and remove any trail back to you. Anything to tie Crist into it?"

"No, but I'm still working on it," Lawrence said.

I got up to remove the steaks from the grill and set them on a foil-covered plate, then covered them with another layer of foil to allow them to continue to cook internally.

"Be right back," I said and entered the trailer where I nuked the steak fries and returned with them two minutes later.

We ate our steaks on TV trays while the tide rolled in and waves crashed against the rocks.

"I didn't ask yet, but what's with the face?" Lawrence said.

I filled him in on recent events.

"You rattled somebody's cage," Lawrence said.

I ate a piece of steak and nodded. The steak was medium, flavorful, and juicy.

"God, I would love to take this off the back burner and run with it," Lawrence said. "See where it goes."

"I thought that's what you were doing," I said.

"Back burner only. I'm just one guy poking around," Lawrence said. "Active, I have twenty-five agents working assignments round the clock."

"Don't forget your fleet of planes," I said.

"Twelve fucking years I waited for another crack at this," Lawrence said.

There was charged excitement in his voice.

"All I've got to do is tie together my getting mugged with whoever killed my witness and my wife from a dozen years ago and you can," I said. "Piece of cake."

"Shit," Lawrence said.

The excitement was gone.

"Yeah, shit," I said.

"Any leads?"

"Just the bumps on my head."

Lawrence sighed. "At least the steak is good."

We took our coffee watching the sun sink below the horizon.

"What now?" Lawrence asked.

I shrugged.

"Yeah," Lawrence said.

Sometimes *yeah* says it all.

29

Around eight thirty the following morning, Walt called from his office.

I was having coffee down at the beach when the phone in my pocket rang. I checked the number first before I answered the call.

"Got a heads-up for you, John," Walt said.

Waves crashed over my bare feet. I lit a cigarette and waited.

"What the hell's that noise?" Walt said.

"Tide rolling in," I said. "I'm standing in it."

"Don't let anything bite your toes," Walt said. "So listen, being the superb cop that I am, I requested the hospital report for my eyes only on any calls inquiring about your condition."

"Somebody called and they told him I was discharged," I said.

"Can't be anybody else but who sent the

three wise men to pay you that visit," Walt said.

"Which means I'll be monitored and possibly visited again," I said.

"I'd leave that place, John," Walt said. "Go stay at the safe house for a while."

"No operating room," I said.

"Want a backup, a couple of off-duty men to hang around?"

"No."

"For God's sake, John."

"I'll be fine," I said. "So listen, I have some news of my own."

I told Walt about the meeting with Paul Lawrence the night before.

"Why am I starting to feel like a small-town cop?" Walt said.

I tossed the cigarette and crushed it into the sand with my bare foot. "How are things at the safe house?"

"Go see for yourself," Walt said.

"Maybe I will."

"Listen, you watch your ass and you watch it close," Walt said.

"Later," I said and clicked off.

I had another mug of coffee and cigarette in my lawn chair, then went in to take a shower and change clothes. I stepped out of the trailer wearing a light summer suit that concealed the Browning in the small of my back.

I doubted I needed the weapon.

Sunlight was my friend.

After dark, I could worry.

Darkness was my enemy.

For now, I started up the Marquis and drove to the safe house.

A seven-year veteran named Dooley met me in the driveway. He was a big kid, not yet thirty, and had that hungry look in his eye that said he wanted to make detective sooner than later.

"The Lieutenant said you might drop by," Dooley said.

"When?"

"Called about an hour ago."

There is something to be said for old partners knowing each other's thoughts and moves. Thing is, I didn't want to trip over Walt in the dark and stub a toe.

"Who's with you on detail?" I said.

"Officer Jackson-Brown," Dooley said. "We're on until four."

"Great."

I found Janet and Mark kicking a soccer ball around in the backyard. Venus Jackson-Brown was close by, keeping watch. Wearing jeans and a pullover shirt, there was no denying her ample figure. The massive hand cannon hung from her right hip. A shotgun leaned against a tree close by.

"Walt said you'd be by this morning," Venus said as I joined her.

"Walt's too smart for his own good," I said.

"What about you, are you too smart for your own good?" Venus said.

I watched Mark kick a shot past Janet that landed near my feet. I picked up the ball and tossed it back to Mark. Oz was nowhere to be found. I assumed he was inside the house somewhere, having a difficult time being sober.

"If I was smart, I wouldn't be in the position I'm in," I said.

"I said smart, not weak," Venus said. "And exactly what position are we talking about?"

I looked at Venus.

"Women always know their competition," she said.

I looked at Janet.

"I didn't know there was a contest," I said.

"That's because you're a man," Venus said.

"My being a man aside, I'm actually here for a reason," I said. "I'd like to visit my daughter. I'd like to take Janet with me."

Venus removed a cell phone from her belt. "I'll need to talk to Walt," she said.

While Venus phoned Walt, I walked to Janet. She was returning a kick to Mark. They paused when I approached.

"Hey, Uncle Jack," Mark said.

"Hey," I said. "I need to borrow your mom for a minute."

"Sure," Mark said. He turned and rolled the ball toward Molly, who was doing her best to be invisible.

Janet and I walked across the backyard.

"Not for nothing," Janet said. "But the next time you have the need to stash me someplace for my own good, don't assign a cop to protect me that has a schoolgirl crush on you."

I threw my hands up.

"Whatever," Janet said.

"I thought I'd go visit Regan," I said.

Janet looked at me.

"I want you to go with me."

Janet nodded. "When?"

"Now if Walt approves it," I said.

We turned to look at Venus. She was returning the phone to her hip.

"Walt said nobody goes anywhere until he shows up," Venus said.

"When?" I said.

"He's on the way right now," Venus said.

"We have time for coffee," Janet said.

Venus, Janet, and I were taking coffee at

the patio table under the awning when Walt arrived with two additional officers.

Dooley, standing watch at the bay window in the living room that faced the street, followed Walt to the backyard.

"Why today?" Walt said to me.

"Coffee?" I said to Walt.

Walt glared at me.

"It's time, that's all," I said.

"Venus, you and Dooley ride with me," Walt said. "I'll have two officers stay here with the boy and the old man. Janet, you best ride with me, too."

Janet looked at Venus.

"We can chat on the way," Venus said.

30

The last time I visited Hope Springs Eternal, I was too drunk to notice the facility was twenty notches above my pay grade.

I don't remember much from that visit, just that Regan was at a table coloring with crayons in a book.

I probably knew but forgot that the entire facility was run by nuns and priests. Most of the nuns were nurses, most of the priests were doctors. It was a mixed bag of psychiatrists and administrators.

We, meaning me, Walt, Venus, and Janet, waited in a large lobby ornate with Catholic artifacts. Dooley stayed outside with the car.

"Place is beautiful," Venus remarked.

Whatever else Eddie Crist was, he wasn't a liar. My daughter had been well cared for in a facility far more expensive than I could ever afford.

Sister Mary Martin entered the lobby and looked at me. "I have to say, Mr. Bekker, that you appear far healthier than your previous visit."

"If you mean sober, I am," I said.

"It's what I meant," the nun said.

"I'm here to see my daughter," I said.

"You can visit Regan in the garden," Sister Mary Martin said.

I touched Janet on the shoulder. "Janet is Regan's aunt," I said. "My wife's sister. I'd like her to go with me."

Sister Mary Martin nodded and we followed her through a maze of hallways to an open courtyard that faced the backyard gardens.

At the archway to the gardens, Father Thomas stepped out to greet me. "Mr. Bekker," the priest said, extending his right hand.

We shook.

"Regan is my patient," Thomas said.

"You're a psychiatrist?" I said.

"Clinical."

"What's the difference?" I said.

"In simplest terms, think of it like this," Thomas said. "Normal persons with some problems to work out make an appointment with a psychiatrist to do that. Regan doesn't even know she has problems."

"Will she ever?" I said.

"I can't answer that," Thomas said. "Yet."

223

"At least you didn't say it's in God's hands."

"Mr. Bekker?" Thomas said.

"Sober as a judge, Father," I said.

"I'll walk you to Regan," Thomas said.

The priest escorted us across the wide gardens to where Regan sat at a table in the shade of an overhanging paper birch tree. She was coloring in a book.

"Regan, your father and aunt are here to visit you," Thomas said.

My daughter didn't so much as bat an eye in my direction.

"Can she hear me?" I said.

"She hears fine," Thomas said. "What she hears and how she perceives it are the mystery."

I sat at the table. Janet sat next to me. We watched Regan color for a minute. She had it down pat, keeping colors and shades in the borders of the pictures so they more resembled photographs than cartoons.

"Does she ever stop?" I asked Thomas.

"When she wants to," Thomas said. "When she's tired or wants to eat."

"Does she know I'm her father?"

"Ask her," Thomas said.

"Regan," I said. "It's Dad. I'm here to see you."

Regan paused with her hand on the

crayon. She didn't look at me, though. She stared at the page in the coloring book.

"Aunt Janet is here with me," I said.

Regan's eyes slowly raised, first to look at Janet, then at me. Her face showed no sign of recognition or emotion.

"Hi, honey," I said.

For a fleeting second, I thought I saw a spark of recognition in Regan's eyes. The second passed. Regan lowered her eyes and continued coloring.

I looked at Janet. Tears were streaming down her cheeks even though she hadn't made a sound.

I touched Janet's hand. She took hold of it and I noticed Regan's eyes shift over to watch our hands come together. When Regan's eyes shifted back to the coloring book, her crayon had gone outside the line on the drawing she was coloring.

Regan sighed, lowered the crayon to the table, stood up, and started walking toward the archway of the facility.

"Going for a new book," Thomas said. "Meticulous, as you can see."

I watched my daughter walk to the archway. She was as tall and shapely as her mother, a beautiful seventeen-year old, budding woman trapped inside the mind of a child.

I looked at the priest.

"I'll try to visit more often," I said.

"If I may make a suggestion," Thomas said. "Bring her a gift. Some new coloring books and crayons with the new colors."

"Will she come back out?" I said.

"After you've gone," Thomas said. "She thinks it's your fault she made a mistake."

Regan entered the facility. "Has she . . . does she ever leave the grounds?"

"Many times," Thomas said. "Trips to the zoo, the circus, museums, and even the movies on occasion. She does appear to enjoy the outings very much."

I nodded.

"Mr. Bekker," Thomas said. "If you want to reconnect with Regan, stay sober."

I nodded again.

It was time to go.

Thomas saw us back to the lobby, where I shook his hand.

"I'll be back in a few days," I said.

Thomas looked at Janet.

"I think it would be a good idea if you came along as well," Thomas said. "She needs other women in the world besides nuns."

"Of course," Janet said.

Walt drove us back to the safe house.

I never wanted a drink so badly in all my life.

31

The late afternoon sun was low in the sky. The beach was cast in an eerie yellowish glow.

I sat in my lawn chair and stared at the unopened bottle of scotch on the card table.

The amber bottle glowed invitingly in the sunlight. An old friend wanting to catch up on what we missed.

The kind of friend not satisfied to hear just one story and say goodbye. The kind of friend who stopped by on a Friday night for a chat and didn't leave until Monday morning.

If I cracked the seal, I knew I was doomed.

I had a mug of coffee in my hand. I took a sip and lit a smoke.

If there was a better combination than coffee and a cigarette, it was a shot and a cigarette.

Today, I would settle for second best.

I made a promise.

Not to the priest, to my daughter, or even myself.

To a dying mobster who took better care of my daughter than I ever could.

It was the kind of promise you kept.

Several mugs of coffee later, I entered the trailer and moved the small coffee table in the living room off the circular rug it rested upon. I tossed the rug aside, grabbed the handle to the trap door, and lifted that.

I stuck my head through the opening. With the trailer suspended three feet off the ground on four wheels and eight cinderblocks, there was plenty of navigation room down below.

I removed the steel case from under the bed, wrapped the M-4 shotgun in a pillowcase, and dropped it down the hole, along with a box of shells.

Then I closed the trapdoor and brewed a fresh pot of coffee.

I was watching a baseball game on the TV from my lawn chair. The sun was long gone; the sky was overcast and dark. Behind me, the trailer was dark and the door was closed.

I reached for the bottle of scotch and cracked the seal. I poured a bit into a water glass. I walked it down to the beach and poured all but a few ounces into the sand, then returned to my seat and rested it on the card table beside the glass.

I watched the game into the seventh inning.

With the game tied at two apiece, I muted the sound and carried a mug of coffee to the trailer. I knelt down and slid the mug under, then rolled into position beside the shotgun.

An hour passed.

I could see the light from the TV, but not much else.

This time they took their car across the beach. They drove without headlights. I watched from under the trailer as the car stopped and the engine shut down. A moment later, three men got out.

They went to the card table.

"Look at this," a man said. "Must be passed out inside if he drank this much."

"Drunk or not, he goes," another of the three said.

One of them opened the door.

The three of them entered the trailer.

I removed the shotgun from the pillowcase and rolled out from under the trailer. I took a position behind the TV and waited.

I didn't have to wait long.

They filed out.

One of them said, "Must be passed out

down by the beach somewhere."

The light from the TV was just bright enough for me to see them. Each man had a silenced pistol in his right hand. Standing in darkness behind the TV, they couldn't see me.

"I'm holding an M-4 semi-automatic shotgun right at you," I said. "I'll take the three of you before you can sight me by voice, so let's make this easy and you put down the guns."

They peered into the darkness, searching for me.

"He's bluffing," one of them said.

"No, I'm not," I said.

"Fan out," another said.

"Don't be stupid," I said. "At this distance, I'll get two of you with one shell."

They were stupid.

Or desperate.

Same result.

In a practiced motion, two fanned out while the third gave cover by firing rounds in my direction.

I blew a hole in the stomach of the one on the left, shifted the M-4 a few inches and shot the one in the middle, firing rounds in the face.

The one on the right stopped fanning and started running.

He was a good runner.

He made it a hundred yards before I caught up with him.

"That's enough of this running," I yelled.

We were separated by less than six feet. I fired a blast into the sand and he stopped running.

"Toss your gun, turn around," I said.

He tossed the pistol and slowly turned around.

I cracked him in the face with the butt of the M-4.

The first thing I found when I searched him was a pair of handcuffs.

The second thing I found was his police badge.

By the time Walt arrived, I was sipping coffee in my lawn chair with a dozen county deputies around me. Jane Morgan, the sheriff leading the posse, sat next to me in the chair usually reserved for Oz. She was also sipping coffee and smoking one of my cigarettes.

Jane was into her fourth elected term as sheriff. She must be doing something right, on the job and at home, because she found the time to be married and raise four sons, two presently in college. We'd crossed paths many times when I was on the job and she knew her stuff. She also took shit from no one.

Walt's car came to a screeching halt beside a deputy cruiser. He jumped out without closing the door and stormed toward my chair.

Jane said, "Oh, my."

I stood up.

"He looks angry," Jane said.

Walt took my shirt in his fists and shoved me backward until I slammed into the wall of the trailer.

"You stupid fuck!" Walt shouted. "What did I tell you, huh? What?"

Jane got out of her chair. "Is that you, Walt?" she said calmly. "What's it been, a few years?"

Walt shook my shirt and slammed my back into the trailer.

"Dumb, stupid, fucking moron," Walt said.

Jane stood beside Walt.

"Well, which is he?" she said. "Dumb, stupid, or a fucking moron. It would be difficult to work all three into one assault report."

Walt looked at Jane.

"Hi, Jane," Walt said.

"Hello, Walt," Jane said. "Maybe you could let him go so we can have a nice chat about what went down here. There's some nice coffee."

Walt let me go.

"Good boy," Jane said.

"Want a cup?" I said.

"You shut up," Walt snapped at me.

We sat in lawn chairs and drank coffee. Jane and I smoked cigarettes.

"So we got two dead and one in a cruiser," Walt said. "Any ID?"

I tossed Walt the man's badge. Walt opened the leather wallet and looked at the badge. *Pleasant City Police Department,* the badge read.

Walt's face went white. Even in the dark I could see it.

"Cops?" Walt said.

"All three of them," Jane said.

"What the fuck?" Walt said.

"About sums it up," Jane said. "Oh good, here's the ME."

The county ME arrived with an ambulance. While he went about his business and the two bodies were bagged and loaded into the ambulance, I refilled mugs with coffee and took my seat.

Walt sipped from his cup. "You could have been killed," he said.

"I wasn't," I said.

"You set them up," Walt said.

"I defended myself against three armed

men here to kill me," I said. "What would you rather I had done?"

"Call me for protection," Walt said.

Jane looked at the cop in the back of her cruiser. "Protect who from whom is the question," she said.

I looked at Jane's cruiser. "What about him?"

Jane looked at Walt. "My jurisdiction, Walt. Care to tag along?"

"Your tag along? This is part of an active, ongoing investigation," Walt said.

"Oh, good," Jane said. "You can tell me about it on the way."

32

"Fuck you, I want my lawyer," Albert Mello said. "And not some shitty PD asshole. Someone from the union."

"Sure, Albert," Jane said. "Right away. As soon as you answer some of my questions."

We were in the interrogation room at the Public Safety Building the sheriff's department called home.

Walt sat next to Jane.

I stood in the background.

"I'm not answering a fucking thing until my lawyer is here," Mello said.

"Oh, dear," Jane said. "I know I'm just a county sheriff and not a big-city cop like you, Albert, but you don't have to be rude."

Mello looked at me.

"Why is he here?" Mello said.

"You tried to murder him," Jane said. "I think that gives him reason, don't you?"

"I think you should shut the fuck up until my lawyer is here," Mello said.

"I checked you out, Albert," Walt said. "Twenty-one years on the job, a dozen citations, solid fitness reports, wife and three kids, so help me out here. What's this all about? Off the record until your lawyer arrives."

"Who the fuck are you?" Mello said.

Walt showed Mello his badge.

"I'm impressed," Mello said. "I'd be even more impressed if you shoved that up your fat ass."

"Must you be so vulgar?" Jane said.

"Look, you stupid bitch," Mello said. "I'll not say it again. I want my fucking lawyer."

Jane sighed.

She stood up.

She removed the Smith & Wesson .40 pistol from her holster and smashed it across Mello's face.

Blood squirted from his nose as Mello fell over backward in his chair.

"Let's see now," Jane said as she holstered the Smith. "How does that thing go again?"

She kicked Mello in the face with a steel-toed boot and more blood squirted.

"You have the right to . . . what is it, now . . . oh yes, remain silent," Jane said.

She kicked Mello in the stomach.

"You have the right to an attorney," she said.

She kicked Mello in the ribs.

"You have the right to be a complete fucking moron," she said.

She kicked Mello in the back.

"A total douche bag, a complete loser, and an asshole to boot," she said.

She kicked Mello in the ribs, the stomach, and the back again.

I looked at Walt. He hadn't moved a muscle.

"Now you're going to talk to us," Jane said. "Because if you don't, I'm going to kick you in the balls and keep kicking you in the balls until they come out your mouth."

Mello looked up at Jane. He was a bloody mess. He spat at her.

Jane kicked him in the balls so hard I felt it in the back of the room.

Mello rolled into a fetal position and held his balls. Silent tears rolled down his face as he gasped for air and cried in between gasps.

"Detective Mello is a bit of a namby pamby," Jane said. "Isn't he, Walt?"

Walt cleared his throat.

It took about five minutes for Mello to regain enough composure to look at Jane.

While we waited, I lit a cigarette. It was against every city and state regulation, but nobody seemed to care in the wake of Jane's tirade, so I happily puffed away.

Jane stood in front of Mello with her steel-tipped boot at the ready. He looked at her. She reared back with the boot.

"Now what the fuck is a detective from a town two hours away doing in my county killing fellow cops, I wonder?" Jane said.

Her boot came forward.

"Stop!" Mello cried.

"Stop?" Jane said.

"Yes, stop," Mello begged. "For God's sake."

Jane looked at Walt. "I think Detective Mello wishes to make a statement at this time," she said.

Walt stood and lifted Mello into his chair, then went and sat back down.

"I don't have a fat ass," Walt told Mello.

Jane also sat and looked at Mello.

"Oh, dear," she said. "You're quite the mess, aren't you?"

"I'm a little fish," Mello said. "In a very big pond. I'll give you the big fish and a dozen more and I walk with complete immunity, plus my pension. Otherwise, we have nothing to talk about."

Jane sighed and looked around the interrogation room. "Now where did I put that state prosecutor?" she said. She waved at the two-way mirror. "Oh, yes," she said.

The door opened and Carly Simms, state attorney general, walked in.

"If you think I'm a bitch," Jane said. "Meet super bitch. Talk to her."

Walt looked at Jane.

"I love you," he said.

Jane shrugged. "I get that a lot."

33

It was the perfect set-up.

Pleasant City is a sleepy little town two hours west and situated six miles from the state border. It had tree-lined streets, beautiful parks for kids to play in, excellent schools, a low unemployment rate, an even lower crime rate, and the most corrupt police department I've ever heard of in my entire life.

Captain Ralph Giraldo ran the show. Twelve of his twenty-four officers were in on it with him, six of the twelve being detectives.

For a hefty fee, Giraldo would make certain problems go away. Arson, extortion, drugs, and murder topped the list of services provided. Clients were mostly mob related, but he had a fair amount in the private sector as well.

Giraldo worked through a middleman he never met and spoke with only on his private line at home. Once he accepted a job, payment was in cash, delivered to a private box at the local post office. He assigned jobs according to the abilities of his twelve. Some were more suited than others for murder, arson, and so on.

According to Mello.

After a lengthy interview with Mello, Carly Simms, Walt, Jane, and I went to breakfast in a diner not far from the beach.

We took a booth.

Simms looked at me.

"Excuse me, but exactly who are you?" she said.

"I'm the victim," I said.

"You blew two of them away with a shotgun and captured the third and you're the victim?" Simms said.

"I didn't say I was a helpless victim," I said.

"Look, Carly," Walt said. "Before you became the big cheese in this state, John Bekker was the best damn cop I ever worked with."

"Was?" Simms said and looked at me. "What are you now?"

"Just a guy who didn't want to get killed," I said.

"And that entitles you to a three-man hit squad how?" Simms said.

"It's complicated," Walt said.

"Simplify it," Simms said.

Over breakfast, Walt and I took turns explaining why I was the focus of a three-man hit squad.

"About the only thing I'm sure of is that Eddie Crist didn't put the hit on me," I said to end my story.

Simms had ordered eggs over easy and was mopping up the yolk with a piece of buttered toast. "Right now I have a hard-on for Giraldo that would make a Mustang stallion blush," she said as she bit into her toast. "Walt, this is related to your case. Jane, you caught this ball. Care to escort me to the judge for warrants?"

"I have a hair appointment at noon," Jane said. "Let me call and reschedule."

Simms looked at Jane's hair.

"Just for a touch-up," Jane said. "A few stray grays."

"Me?" I said.

Simms turned to me.

"He's earned it," Walt said. "Without him, we wouldn't be having this party."

"Background music only," Simms said.

Mello sang like a pet store full of canaries. The judge jumped at the chance to sign warrants, but cautioned Simms the media was not to be alerted until after Giraldo was in custody.

The siege on the Pleasant City Police Department unfolded at four in the afternoon.

Jane contacted the sheriff's department in the next county and had two dozen deputies assigned to her. She brought a dozen of her own. Walt borrowed six state police officers in full SWAT gear.

Simms ran the show.

I stayed in the background.

Giraldo was at his desk when the swarm of cops, led by Simms, entered the Pleasant City Police Department and took command. Giraldo appeared dazed and confused as state police handcuffed him while Jane read him his rights.

"You caused me to miss my hair appointment," Jane said to Giraldo.

"What?" Giraldo said.

"Be grateful you're not in her interrogation room," Walt told Giraldo.

In all, we left with Giraldo and nine of his men in handcuffs.

Jane appointed a sergeant who was ignorant of Giraldo's activities as acting chief until the matter was sorted out at a later time.

After eight hours of questioning, it became

clear Giraldo was telling the truth that he had no idea who placed the contract on me.

"I never know," Giraldo said. "It's just a voice on the phone and it's never from the same phone twice. I check the numbers. He uses a disposable cell phone. It could be anybody from anywhere."

"Your payments?" Simms said.

"Same," Giraldo said. "He has a key to my post office box. The money is there after a job. I go and pick it up."

"You picked it up?" Simms said.

Giraldo nodded.

"You ever try to find the source?" Simms said.

"No," Giraldo said. "And I don't want to know."

"Too bad," Simms said. "Because now you have nothing to bargain with."

"Not necessarily," I said.

I was standing against the wall, silent up until now.

Simms, Jane and Walt turned to look at me.

I walked to the table and stood behind Walt.

"You have something to say?" Simms said.

"What if in exchange for his cooperation, Giraldo was to receive a lesser charge and sentence?" I said. "Sent to a country club for fifteen years with early out."

Giraldo looked at me. "I'm listening."

"How often do you get contacted?" I said.

"Every week, couple of times a month," Giraldo said. "No way of predicting."

"What if we allowed Giraldo to return to work as usual until the next call?" I said. "And we staked out the post office for the deliveryman. If the deliveryman and Giraldo testify before a grand jury, you could crack an ostrich egg instead of a chicken egg."

Simms looked at me, turned, and looked at Giraldo.

"Would you go for that?" Simms said.

"I keep my pension when I'm released," Giraldo said. "Or no deal."

"Let's go talk to the judge," Simms said.

Giraldo looked at me. "Who are you?"

"I'm the victim," I said. "The guy you tried to kill."

34

Walt said, "So who doesn't want you among the living anymore and how is that connected to Crist?"

"Maybe the deliveryman can tell us?" I said.

"Somebody way back, say twelve years ago, wanted you out of the way," Walt said. "You went away basically on your own, so let sleeping dogs sleep. Except that you woke up and now you have to go away again. Why?"

We were in Walt's office. We each had a mug of coffee and a donut from Pat's.

"I'm in the way," I said.

"Of what?"

I bit into my donut, a raspberry cream. Raspberry jelly ran down my chin. I wiped it with a finger and licked it off.

"Somebody's freedom," I said. "Freedom is a powerful motive if it's threatened."

Walt tore into his donut, swallowed, and

sipped coffee. "My life was a lot easier when you were on the sauce," he said.

"Funny," I said. "Somewhere, somebody else is saying the exact same thing."

I stood up.

"Where you going?" Walt said.

"I'm taking what's left of my delicious donut over to see Crist," I said.

"Tell him hi for me," Walt said. "But don't tell him I got odds on him in the dead pool."

Crist met me in the backyard by the pool. It was a warm evening with a slight easterly breeze. The floodlights made it appear close to daylight. I could see the gauntness in his face, the frailness in his thin shoulders.

Four wingtips took up position around the pool, close enough if needed, too far away to eavesdrop.

Crist had coffee served from a silver tray and matching pot.

"What do you know about Captain Giraldo and the Pleasant City Police Department?" I said and sipped coffee from a silver cup.

"My faith in you is justified," Crist said.

I pulled my cigarette pack and looked at Crist. He nodded and I lit up.

"Back in the late unpleasantness of the

mid-eighties, when that asshole in New York took power, we needed a new way to do business," Crist said. "Accountants and lawyers run the show now. The public has no taste for what goes on behind the scenes. We solved our little PR problem by recruiting police departments across the country to do the dirty work for us. It's not difficult to get some slob making thirty-five thousand a year to pop some goon or torch a building for fifty grand a shot. Pleasant City is one of my first recruits going back twenty years. Giraldo was nothing but a sergeant back then. I bought him his bars and plenty of others."

"Anything to tie you in?" I said.

"There's so many buffers involved, my daughter will be a hundred by the time they figure them all out," Crist said. "The idea of using cops as hit men came about after the mess they made of your witness twelve years ago and . . . your wife. Michael put it all together, actually. Up until then, we used the cops for information mostly and the occasional lean on some asshole trying to muscle their way in where they don't belong. It couldn't have been cops back then because we hadn't recruited them for the heavy lifting yet."

"It was Giraldo who sent them to kill me

the other night," I said.

"Giraldo wouldn't know you from a hole in the wall," Crist said. "It went through several layers of buffers before it reached him. I know it wasn't me or anybody connected to me who gave the order. My guess is it's somebody connected to your past that thinks you're getting a little too close for comfort. Somebody who still has knowledge and connections."

"And that somebody is?"

"Any one of a dozen or more on the coast alone," Crist said. "Could be organization or it could be private sector. All I can tell you is, the order didn't come from me. A half dozen families inside the organization use the system as well, but generally a move isn't made without my knowledge."

"Generally?" I said.

"Nothing's perfect."

"Can you find out who gave the order and made the payment?"

"I'll have Kagan make some inquiries," Crist said.

"Thank you."

"Don't," Crist said. "It's too much to hope for that the same man who ordered the hit is the man who killed your wife. Nothing is ever that easy or that obvious."

"Maybe not, but there's a connection and

connections tend to leave a trail of bread-crumbs if you know how and where to look," I said.

"Ironic though, isn't it?" Crist said. "That the man who once built a case against me is the same man I hired to find his wife's killer, and he gets a contract on him from the organization I helped create."

"Life is full of surprises," I said.

"I have the feeling I can say the same thing about death," Crist said.

We were silent for a moment.

I smoked my cigarette.

"Just because Michael didn't use the cops to kill my witness and Carol doesn't mean he wasn't behind it," I said.

"I know," Crist said. "So you still have some work to do."

I nodded.

"I visited my daughter the other day," I said. "It's different when your mind is clear. She's beautiful like her mother, and meticulous like her mother, too."

"But no words?"

"No."

"She will," Crist said. "When she has something worthwhile to say. In the meantime all you can do is love her. Like I do with Campbell."

I looked past the lights at the sky. The

moon was waxing behind a thick cover of clouds, illuminating them against a backdrop of night.

Crist looked at it, too.

"My time is almost up," he said. "When I get to hell and meet my son, I'd like to know he isn't there because of your wife."

How do you respond to that?

I didn't.

35

Sometimes things just nag at you to be seen. You look at something over and over again and just don't see it.

I sat at my kitchen table in the trailer and stared at my handwritten notes.

What had I written that was worth killing me for?

What had I written that I didn't see, that was somehow the key that unlocked the mystery?

To my wife's murder.

To the contract on me a dozen years later.

I drank some coffee, smoked some cigarettes, and read my notes through one more time. I saw nothing worth killing or dying for.

Around two in the morning, after nearly two days without sleep, I succumbed to exhaustion and flopped into bed.

I fell into a deep sleep, which is a lot different than passing out.

Eleven hours later, I woke up, which is a lot different than coming to.

I brewed some coffee, then made breakfast of an omelet with grilled English muffins and jam.

I sat and looked at my notes again.

I put them away and ate my breakfast.

I thought about Regan, how meticulously she colored in her books, how upset with herself she became when a crayon made a mark outside the line.

I looked at the page and saw a crayon mark.

Regan looked at the same page and saw something entirely different.

Regan looked outside the box.

I did not.

Armed with a fresh pot of coffee, I gathered my stack of notes and took my seat at the lawn chair. For once, the beach was devoid of gulls. The tide was out. The waves were calm.

I read.

I drank coffee and smoked cigarettes.

I read again.

After a long time, I set the stacks of paper on the card table and closed my eyes.

Who benefited by removing me from the investigation?

I opened my eyes and lit a smoke.

Who benefited so much they would risk the FBI and police department hounding them like dogs on a squirrel?

I walked down to the beach and looked at the calm, blue waters for a while.

Who was/is smart enough to outsmart the FBI and police department?

Some gulls flying around thought my presence on the beach would mean a free meal. They landed nearby and squawked at me for food.

Whoever benefited the most killed my wife.

"Everybody need a reason," Oz said weeks ago.

Carol was killed for a reason. Find the reason and find whoever killed her.

The gulls squawked at me with open beaks, waiting for some free tidbits.

A page from my notes jumped into my mind.

I raced back to my chair, grabbed the stack of papers and flipped through them until I found that page.

A list of Michael Crist's bodyguards who gave depositions to Lewis and Clark and agreed to take polygraph tests.

Two lists, actually.

One of Michael Crist's personal bodyguards in Las Vegas. The second of Michael Crist's personal bodyguards back home where he lived with his father and kept a small apartment in town.

Thirteen names in all.

Six for Vegas, six for home, one as a traveling companion.

One name, one man, traveled with Michael in both locations.

Carlo Starace, known as Charlie Stars, according to Clark's bio information. His occupation was listed as professional bodyguard. His age would be forty-four today. His specs were six foot four, two forty in weight.

A big fellow.

Certainly big enough to handle my wife the way she was murdered.

Beside his name was a one-inch square black and white photograph. The definition was grainy, but good enough to see Charlie was a handsome fellow in a cruel sort of way.

Cruel enough to do what had to be done?

As any woman will tell you, if you want to know about the man you're dating, check out his friends.

As any cop will tell you, if you want to know about a suspect, check out how he makes his living.

Friends and money tell you all you need to know.

36

David Clark was coaching the son of a wealthy banker on giving testimony on the witness stand when I arrived at his office. The son was accused of the first-degree murder of his girlfriend after a night of drinking and drugs with friends. Over breakfast at a local IHOP, an argument broke out when the son accused his girlfriend of flirting with the man who waited on their table.

The son stabbed the girlfriend to death in the IHOP parking lot with an IHOP steak knife. Clark's case hinged upon the drugs and booze being responsible for the murder and not the son, who was a victim himself of clouded judgment.

Good luck with that one.

I read a magazine in the waiting room while Clark finished up with the son.

After a while, a receptionist came to usher me into Clark's office.

"You've either uncovered some missing detail or you're bored for some good conversation," Clark said. "Which?"

I took the chair opposite his desk.

"Carlo Starace," I said. "Also known as Charlie Stars."

"What in God's name are you talking about?" Clark said.

"You interviewed and administered a polygraph to Michael Crist's entire bodyguard staff twelve years ago," I said. "Michael had a staff in Vegas and another here at home. Carlo Starace is the only man who served on both."

"So?"

"If he traveled with Michael, it means he had a deeper relationship, friendship, and trust than the others," I said. "Which means he may know more than what came up at your depositions."

Clark sat back in his chair and looked at me.

"I cede your point," Clark said. "What do you want to do about it twelve years after the fact?"

"Do you have records of his poly test?" I said. "And other background info you gathered in case of a trial."

Clark sighed. "I'll have to send out to our storage facility," he said. "Can you come

258

back around five this afternoon?"

I looked at my watch.

"I'll be back," I said.

Walt said, "Who's this fucking guy and why should I stay on unpaid overtime to find out?" as he looked at the bio information I set on his desk that Clark dug up at his storage facility.

"Michael Crist's personal bodyguard," I said.

"Michael Crist had a lot of bodyguards," Walt said.

"Carlo Starace is the only one who traveled with Michael from Vegas to home and back," I said. "This guy was inner circle. Inner circle guys have more trust. Inner circle guys know more than those on the fringe. I'd like to know what the more is."

Walt looked at the bio.

He looked at me.

"As it just so happens, I needed Venus in records today," Walt said. "Let's go see what she can tell us."

Venus was checking a wants and warrants call for a cop in the field when we entered her domain.

We waited for her to finish the call.

Venus hung up her phone, spun her chair around, and looked at us. Me, really.

"I knew you'd come begging for something," Venus said.

Walt looked at me.

"I need a favor," I said.

"A favor implies a debt is owed," Venus said.

Walt looked at Venus.

"What the hell is this?" Walt said. "The freaking Bachelor?"

Venus looked at Walt. "What do you need?"

Walt gave Venus the sheet of paper I gave him. She scanned it quickly. "Who is Carlo Starace?" she said.

"Used to work for Michael Crist as his personal bodyguard," Walt said.

"What's he do now?" Venus said.

"We were sort of hoping you could tell us," I said.

Venus got busy pushing buttons and clicking the mouse on her computer. After about fifteen minutes, she said, "Carlo Starace, age forty-four, resides in Las Vegas. Has a Vegas-issued driver's license, pistol permit, and business license. No arrest record, wants, or warrants. One speeding ticket from nine years ago, paid the fine. Two parking tickets from seven and four years ago, paid the fines. Otherwise, he's clean."

"What kind of business license?" I said.

Venus clicked the mouse a few more times.

"Runs a whorehouse outside the Vegas city limits where it's legal," Venus said. "Calls it an escort club for gentlemen." Venus looked at me.

"That address on the license current?"

"Yes, it is. Planning a trip?" Venus said.

"Maybe."

"To pay for something there you can get for free right here?" Venus said.

Walt tossed up his hands. "My office," he said.

We returned to Walt's office.

"What do you think?" I said.

"I think Carlo Starace knows more than your average bodyguard," Walt said. "How much more and about what is the question. What about Crist, you talk to him?"

"Crist told me Michael handled his own affairs," I said. "Contracted his own protection and street soldiers. Crist probably never even met Starace, except for maybe in passing."

"You going to Vegas?"

"Yes."

"Let me see that Mickey Mouse PI license of yours."

I dug out my wallet.

Walt studied the ID and gave the wallet back to me.

"I know the Vegas police chief," Walt said. "I'll call him and let him know you'll be operating in his town, but you check in with him on arrival."

"Sure."

"Don't sure me, asshole," Walt said. "Last time you said sure, you killed two cops who tried to kill you."

"Speaking of which, anything new on Giraldo?" I said.

"He's at home," Walt said. "They tapped his phones waiting for the next call."

"Maybe we'll get lucky," I said.

"I think if you go downstairs to records you'll get lucky," Walt said.

"I have no time for women," I said.

"Who does?" Walt said.

37

I was watching the Baltimore Orioles get the snot beat out of them by the Yankees in a humid night game in The Bronx and thinking about Carlo Starace. Mostly thinking about Starace and his connection to Carol's death.

Was there one?

It was entirely possible that as a member of Michael Crist's inner circle Starace knew, or at least knew how to employ, Fagan Cavanaugh, if it was Cavanaugh who bombed my witness.

A million dollars is a lot of money.

An average working stiff has to work twenty-five years to earn a million, pre-taxes. That's a lot of years.

A casino owned by the Crist family makes that in a day.

So Cavanaugh bombs my witness with C-4, his trademark. Who came to my home to deliver the message, found I wasn't there, and took it out on Carol?

Not Cavanaugh's style.

He didn't do hands-on.

He liked to observe his work from a distance and relive the glory of the event on the news.

Carlo Starace, on the other hand, was a professional bodyguard to Michael Crist and it doesn't get more hands-on than that.

Say Starace wanted to deliver the message to me personally after the bombing, thought I was home when I wasn't, and surprised Carol in the shower.

As a theory, it worked.

As evidence to the crime, it didn't.

Too many missing pieces of the puzzle. I needed to buy some vowels to solve it. Where was Vanna White when you needed her?

My cell phone rang. I grabbed it off the card table and answered the call.

"Giraldo took a call from a mobster in Rhode Island," Walt said. "Wants a labor dispute on the docks cleared up. Wants some union rep talking strike to go bye-bye."

"Who knew Rhode Island had a coast," I said.

"It does, asshole," Walt said. "So three FBI guys acting as Giraldo's cops will pick up the union rep and stash him someplace safe until the drop is made. You want to hang with me on the stakeout?"

"When?"

"Post office opens at eight-thirty tomorrow morning," Walt said.

"Who else is in?" I said.

"Some of my guys, Jane Morgan's people, and Carly Simms as a ride along," Walt said.

"You're sure that's enough people to take down one guy opening a post office box?" I said.

"You have something better to do?" Walt said.

"Fly to Vegas," I said.

It was a dark, moonless night and the twin lights in the distance stuck out on the beach like a lighthouse.

"Fly to Vegas the day after," Walt said. "The captain's back and I'm softening him up to go with you on a junket if I can make the case."

No mistaking the twin lights as belonging to a car.

"Want me to talk to him?" I said.

"Did I mention I wanted to go?"

The car lights veered toward my trailer. The car was moving slow. The driver was unsure of his destination.

"I'll meet you at five-thirty," I said.

"Dress for the occasion," Walt said.

I hit end, set the phone on the card table, and went inside for the M-4 shotgun. I returned to my chair and rested it against my leg.

From the small of my back, I removed the Browning and set it on the card table next to my smokes.

The car slowed near Oz's trailer, paused for a moment, then turned and made its way toward me. I shielded my eyes with my left hand so as not to lose my night vision and placed my right hand on the shotgun.

The car stopped and parked next to the Marquis.

The lights turned off and the door opened.

Venus Jackson-Brown stepped out of the car and walked toward me. She was still in uniform.

"You won't need that," Venus said, motioning to the shotgun. "At least I think you won't."

I put the shotgun on the card table.

"What are you doing here?" I said.

Venus looked at the trailer behind me. "I had a hell of a time finding this place and you know perfectly well what I'm doing here."

"Want some coffee while we discuss this?" I said.

"I want a big fat rum and Coke is what I want, but I'll settle for a coffee," Venus said. "Provided it's strong."

I fetched two mugs.

Venus sipped.

I lit a smoke.

"I'm here because we both want this," Venus said. "I know about you and the sister-in-law and all that. This ain't about that. This is about the sexual tension between us that we need to put to rest. This is a one-time offer, a one-time deal. I don't have room in my life for mutts like you."

"I hate being sweet-talked," I said.

Venus grinned and sipped coffee. "You got a shower in that dump? I could use a shower first."

I nodded.

"Large enough for two?"

I nodded.

Venus put her cup on the ground.

"Let's go," Venus said.

From my bed, I watched Venus put on her uniform. She was one hundred and forty-eight pounds of solid muscle. She had a wide, flaring back, powerful shoulders, and ropes for arms.

"Now we can go back to our humdrum lives and not think about the what-if question hanging over our heads," Venus said as she buttoned her shirt.

"That what-if we did twice nearly killed me," I said.

"That what-if was pretty damn good," Venus said. "Both times."

I sat up on the bed with my feet on the floor. "What's good for a leg cramp?"

"You're not that old, Bekker," Venus said as she strapped on her holster and utility belt. "I can attest to that. Both times."

Venus sat down next to me and rested her head on my shoulder. "If I didn't have all those damn kids and you weren't so fucked up in the head, maybe there would be something more between us than a hole in one, but I do and you are. So think of this as a confidence builder for your sister-in-law."

"Great," I said.

Venus kissed me on the cheek. "Gotta go," she said. "The sitter is on overtime."

I tossed on a robe and followed Venus outside. She entered her car and drove away. I flopped in my lawn chair and watched.

As her taillights faded away, I lit a cigarette and thought about Carlo Starace.

Venus referred to our lovemaking as what-if.

That's what Carlo Starace was, a giant what-if.

What if he, acting on orders from Michael, made contact with Cavanaugh to murder my witness twelve years ago? And what if he was behind the message delivered to my wife? And what if I somehow could prove all this?

What would I do?

I went to bed, set the alarm clock for four, and stared at the black ceiling while I smelled the hint of perfume left behind by Venus.

I felt guilty for cheating on my sister-in-law. I felt guilty for cheating on my wife with my sister-in-law.

I felt guilty for being alive and my wife wasn't.

"I'm coming to get you, Carlo," I said and rolled my face into the pillow to grab two hours' sleep.

38

The perfect place to keep close surveillance on the post office was from inside a post office truck parked in the post office parking lot across the street from it. A wireless remote camera mounted on the side mirror displayed the front door, sidewalk, and windows of the post office in beautiful, HD color.

A second wireless remote camera was tucked neatly into the overhead fluorescent light fixture in the post office box room in the post office lobby. It also displayed in HD color on the two monitors inside the truck.

An industrial DVD recorder that cost somebody seven grand rested on a small stand. It had the capability of recording to memory or disc and could play back in real time or two-second intervals. It could also enhance and develop still photos in under ten seconds.

We took positions one hour before the post office opened, which gave us plenty of time for coffee and donuts from Pat's. There were just the four of us — Walt, Jane, Carly Simms, and myself — inside the truck, but we went through the dozen donuts the way baseball players go through sunflower seeds.

Outside the van in an extended perimeter were a dozen deputies in plain clothes and unmarked vehicles and six detectives from Walt's squad, also in unmarked vehicles. They took positions at parking meters, down a one-way side street, at intersections to block the possibility of a getaway car, and in the parking lot beside the rear street exit.

We waited.

We watched.

We ate donuts and drank coffee.

The first hour passed without incident.

Traffic into and out of the post office was light to moderate. People mailing packages and buying stamps, some retrieving their mail from their boxes, but nobody went near Giraldo's allotted box.

"This is fucking boring," Simms said.

"It's only been an hour," Walt said.

"These things take time," Jane said. "Weeks, sometimes."

"Relax, Carly," Walt said. "It will happen

today if all goes to pattern."

I lit a cigarette and set the pack on the counter beside the keyboard.

Simms freaked out.

"What the fuck is wrong with you?" she snapped. "We're in a closed environment here."

I looked at Simms.

"It's vented," I said.

"At least have the common courtesy to move to the rear so the rest of us don't have to breathe your vile secondhand smoke," Simms snapped at me.

Walt looked at Simms.

"Recently quit, huh?" he said.

Simms stared at Walt for a moment. Then, with catlike reflexes, she snared my pack and lit up.

"Don't you say a fucking word," Simms snarled at me.

"Isn't that Clair Tremont from the local news?" Jane said. "I didn't know she lived around here."

On the monitor we watched an attractive-looking woman in a mini-skirted power suit enter the post office.

"Yeah," Simms said. "And if that skirt was any shorter, I could see her bikini wax."

"I like what she's done to her hair, though," Jane said.

"Yeah, except I can see her roots from here," Simms said as she blew smoke through her nose like an angry dragon.

Jane looked at Simms.

"Yours looks fine, though," Simms said.

Walt sighed as he looked at me.

Early morning turned into late morning.

People came and went, some with parcels, some to pick up their mail, some just buying stamps. Nobody went near the targeted post office box. It was all, as Simms said, fucking boring.

That's what ninety percent of police work is, really. Mundane tasks, followed by the routine, ending in the tedious.

Just like on TV and in the movies.

Around noon, I noticed Simms crossed her legs in her chair.

"What do you do if you have to pee?" Simms said.

"You pee," Walt said.

"In?" Simms said.

"You don't do a lot of stakeouts, do you, dear?" Jane said as she reached down and produced an empty coffee can.

Simms eyed the can.

"How does that work?" she said. "I can't exactly whip it out."

"Oh, well, see what you do is drop your pants and panties to your ankles and

273

straddle the can like so," Jane said, stood, and demonstrated by placing the can between her thighs. "You can grip with your thighs if . . ."

"With these two watching?" Simms said.

"You won't watch, will you boys?" Jane said.

"No," Walt said.

"Wouldn't dream of it," I said.

Simms took the can.

"Make sure they don't peek," Simms said.

"We're cops, we don't peek," Walt said.

"You're men," Simms said. "On your deathbed, you'll peek."

"What if I gave you cover?" Jane said. "You stand in back there and I'll cover you so they can't see."

Simms nodded. She and Jane went to the rear of the truck, about fifteen feet away where Jane shielded Simms from view.

Walt and I concentrated on the monitor.

After sixty seconds of nothing, Jane said, "What's the matter, dear?"

"They can hear," Simms said. "I can't go with them listening."

"For God's sake, prosecutor," Walt said.

"What if we hum?" Jane said. "Do you know the Marine Corps Hymn?"

"How do I wash my hands?" Simms said.

"I have wet naps," Jane said.

While Jane and Simms softly hummed three verses of "From the Halls of Montezuma," Walt ran his fingers through his hair and I watched the monitor.

That was the highlight of the day.

Around ten of four, Simms said, "What time is Giraldo making the pickup?"

"Four-thirty," Walt said. "That's when the post office closes, but the lobby stays open until seven. An overnight sorter locks it then."

"If this is a no show, I'm going to squeeze Giraldo's balls until they pop like cherry tomatoes," Simms said.

"Besides the post office manager, who else is in on this?" Simms said.

"Nobody," Walt said. "Not the clerks or the drivers. Just him."

Simms chain-smoked my cigarettes the final forty minutes. At four-thirty, a clerk locked the interior lobby door, leaving the outer lobby open.

Giraldo's car came into view and parked at the curb beside the post office. He exited with a key dangling on a chain in his right hand.

We watched as Giraldo entered the post office lobby, went to his box, opened it with the key, and removed a thick envelope. He closed the box, removed the key, and stuck the envelope into his inside suit pocket.

"Son of a bitch," Walt said.

"There's no way we missed the drop," Jane said. "No way."

Giraldo exited the lobby, returned to his car, and gave the signal by lowering his window.

"How the fuck did we miss it?" Simms said.

"You didn't," I said. "It came by mail. A sorter put it into the box from the inside where we didn't plant a camera."

"So my two-hour drive isn't wasted, let's go talk to Giraldo before he opens the envelope," Walt said.

Walt inspected the envelope carefully before opening it. "Addressed to Giraldo with no return address," he said. "Mailed locally."

Simms looked across her desk at Giraldo.

"Ever have the drop mailed before?" Simms said.

Giraldo shifted his weight in his chair. "No."

Walt picked up a letter opener from the desk and carefully sliced open the thick envelope. He removed three stacks of bills and set them on the desk.

"Seventy-five thousand?" Walt said.

Giraldo nodded yes.

"Two possibilities here," Walt said. "One is that they decided to change the MO of the buffer and switch to using U.S. mail. Two is we have a leak somewhere in our case."

"I'm dishonest, not stupid. I'm looking at thirty years if I don't make a deal, you think I'm going to leak?" Giraldo said.

"No," Walt said. "But this whole cop for hire thing was started by Eddie Crist and the mob, so maybe they have people on the inside we don't know about. People on the payroll we talk to everyday who are actually mob informants."

I picked up the envelope and looked at the postmark seal.

"It's a local cancellation seal," I said. "It was probably dropped into the box right in front of the post office last night so it would be picked up first thing this morning."

"Right under our fucking noses," Simms said. "And that fucking Crist walks again. Christ, I hate that old fuck."

"Walt is right, this is from the inside," I said.

Walt sighed at my meaning.

"Jane, you need to do a check on every deputy in your house," Walt said. "In the field and at corrections. Bank accounts, wire transfers, the works. Carly, you too. Everyone who works here, reports to you, the works. I know my house is clean, but I'll do the same."

Every cop's nightmare.

Investigating your own.

I tossed a baseball in the backyard with Mark while Janet kept busy in the kitchen with dinner. Two of Walt's cops kept a close eye on the boy. Another two stayed in the house to watch the street.

"I've been working on my cutter," Mark said. "Want to see?"

"Fire away," I said.

The boy went into a windup and fired a seventy-mile an hour cutter that rose high and to the left. I snared it and tossed it back.

"More snap on the wrist and aim for low and away," I said. "Most hitters can tag a cutter that doesn't move."

Mark nodded. His next pitch came in low and cut away from the plate at the last second.

"Not bad," I said.

Janet slid open the kitchen door. "Boys," she said. "Dinner."

"Aw, mom," Mark complained.

"It doesn't get dark for two hours," Janet said. "You can practice some more after we eat."

Mark looked at me. "You'll stay?"

"Sure."

We filed past Janet into the kitchen.

"All night?" Janet said to me.

"Yeah, Uncle Jack," Mark said. "There's plenty of extra bedrooms and these guys never sleep. We could get an early start in the morning."

"I'm flying to Las Vegas at five in the morning on business," I said. "I don't think it would be a good idea."

"Why not?" Mark said.

"Yeah," Janet said. "Why not?"

"Well, for one thing, I don't have any luggage with me," I said. "For another, from here to the airport is an extra forty-five minutes' drive. I'd have to leave here at two-thirty in the morning."

"You don't have to sleep," Janet said, looking at me.

"Yeah, we can watch TV until it's time for you to leave," Mark said.

Janet looked at Mark. "Nice try, buster. Go wash your hands." She turned to me. "You, too."

Janet and I sipped coffee at the backyard

patio table while Mark rolled a ball of string with Molly on the lawn.

"I don't know what's wrong with me," Janet said softly. "I need you in my bed. It's like I'm having a middle-aged meltdown or something."

"Middle age starts at fifty-five," I said. "So they tell me."

"Only if I live to a hundred and ten," Janet said.

I was itching for a smoke, but the no smoking around Mark rule was in effect.

"What is it?" Janet said.

"Guilt," I admitted.

"I thought we had this conversation," Janet said. "You said you didn't feel guilty."

"I didn't then," I said. "I do now."

"Why?"

"I loved Carol," I said. "She was the best thing that ever happened to me."

"She felt the same way, Jack," Janet said. "After she had that fling, she was beside herself with worry that you'd find out and leave her. She would have been devastated if you had. I know. It was my shoulder she cried on."

Molly had the ball of string in her front paws and beat on it with her back legs. Mark sat beside her and laughed.

"Sixteen years ago Thanksgiving," I said.

"We had it at your house, remember?"

Janet thought for a moment. "Yes. What about it?"

"Your girls were young, Regan was just a baby," I said. "We had dinner at that big table you have in the dining room. You wore a plain skirt to the knee and a green sweater to the neck. Your hair was longer then and you had it pinned back in some kind of Victorian bun. I couldn't keep my eyes off you. I kept looking, trying not to get caught, but I couldn't help myself. I wanted you and I felt guilty about it then and I do now."

"Nothing happened then," Janet said. "You're attaching guilt to thought. By those standards, everyone in the world would be on a psychiatrist's couch, including the psychiatrists. So here's the bottom line, Jack. I'm forty-six years old and ready for a relationship and I want it to be with you. I think you want the same thing, but your guilt is standing in the way. Get rid of it."

"How?"

"Be who you are and do what you do," Janet said. "Find who murdered Carol and you'll forgive yourself for allowing it to happen. Then we can go from there. You see I'm right, don't you?"

I nodded.

"In the meantime, I'm going up to my

room to soak in a hot bath," Janet said. "If you could see your way clear to back-burning your guilt for an hour, maybe you could quietly slip away to join me. I might even let you smoke."

Janet stood up and entered the house through the sliding doors.

I sat for a moment and thought.

Then I stood up and followed Janet up to her bedroom.

At least I'd be clean for the plane ride.

40

Crist's expense money paid for two first-class, round-trip tickets to Las Vegas.

Walt took the window seat. I settled for the aisle where there was enough room to toss a Frisbee. We took off at five-twelve, a few minutes later than scheduled. The pilot assured us we would make up the time in the air. The moment the seat belt sign went off, a steward rolled out the breakfast tray.

"Never flew first class," Walt said as we ate breakfast.

I sipped coffee from a plastic cup. "Refresh my memory as to why you're accompanying me," I said.

"Keep you out of trouble," Walt said. "Alone, you're just a PI down on his luck. Alone, you have no authority to do anything, especially out of state. Alone, you might be tempted to sample the temptations offered by such a place as Vegas. I, on the other hand, am a well-respected lieutenant of the law with connections you don't have. I can open doors you can't. Therefore, you need and require me to accompany you on this fact-finding trip."

"And it has nothing to do with the fact that you're a closet Celine Dion junkie and that she just happens to be performing in Vegas and that you just happen to have tickets in your jacket pocket," I said.

Walt looked at me.

"I saw them when you showed your boarding pass," I said.

Walt continued to look at me.

"I won't mention it to anybody," I said. "Your secret is safe with me."

Walt faced front. "The legs on that woman," he muttered.

After breakfast, I took a nap. I woke up in time to experience the feather-like landing at McCarran International in Las Vegas.

After retrieving our luggage, we grabbed a cab to police headquarters on Sunrise Avenue. The Vegas PD is the Sheriff's Department. There is one sheriff, an undersheriff as second in command, a bunch of assistant sheriffs, and a horde of deputies. Walt had called ahead and made an appointment with the sheriff.

Walt checked his weapon with a deputy in the lobby and we were escorted to the top floor office of Sheriff Daniels, a man of about our age, whippet thin with a nice-looking mustache. With him was Undersheriff Williams, a large black man who resembled a younger Sidney Poitier from the sixties.

"What's it been, five years?" Daniels said as he came across his desk to shake Walt's hand.

"Since the convention," Walt said.

"Don't remind me," Daniels said. "Nothing worse than a bunch of drunken cops loose on the strip. This is Williams, my next in line."

"Pleasure," Williams said.

"You must be John Bekker," Daniels said. "Walt filled me in when we spoke on the phone. Let's talk at the table."

We moved to a conference table centered in the large office where coffee, tea, fresh fruit, and muffins waited.

"Do you plan to carry a weapon?" Daniels said to me.

"Yes," I said. "It's in my luggage. My permit to carry is reciprocal to Nevada."

Daniels nodded. "We checked. We also checked Carlo Starace and he's clean. He wouldn't have been given a license for that cathouse he operates otherwise. Same for his liquor license."

"Clean doesn't mean innocent," I said.

"We know about his involvement with Michael Crist," Daniels said.

"As much as we dislike organized crime, the Crist family operates strictly by the book in Vegas," Williams said. "Even their charity foundation is all above board, legal and actually does a lot of good in the community."

"Starace held a legal license to act as a professional bodyguard, including weapons permits," Daniels said. "We couldn't find one thing to even question him about when Michael Crist was killed. You might find it less than fruitful when you talk to him."

"In that case, Walt has Celine Dion tickets for tomorrow night," I said.

Daniels grinned. "Isn't that where you . . ."

"Never mind," Walt said.

"What?" I said.

"It's a story for another time," Walt said.

"Ever make any arrests in Michael's murder?" I said.

"No," Daniels said. "It's very difficult to arrest somebody when they've disappeared off the face of the Earth."

"Every ranking member of the Campo crime family simply vanished," Williams said. "We knew who was behind Michael

Crist's murder and we knew who was behind the Campo mass exit, but without proof, without evidence to back up our belief . . ." Williams tossed his hands in the air.

"There's a lot of bodies buried out there in the desert," Daniels said. "There's also a whole lot of desert."

Walt nodded. "Do you want daily reports?"

"Only if you have something worth reporting," Daniels said. "Oh, and Walt, enjoy Celine. Her skirts are shorter than ever this year. The legs on that woman."

We took a cab from police headquarters to our hotel a block off the strip. The grass needed mowing. The picket fence needed painting. There was a pool not in use at the moment.

"What a difference a block makes, huh," Walt said.

We dumped our bags in our room, then walked to the strip where we rented a car at an Avis. From there we drove straight to the Gentlemen's Escort and Sports Club.

Walt drove.

I read the map and recited directions.

41

Prostitution is illegal inside the city limits of Las Vegas, but perfectly legal inside the boundaries of Nye County, which is where the largest of Starace's three brothels was located.

The remaining two were north and west about sixty miles, but as Starace's residence was on the premises of the Gentlemen's Escort and Sports Club, that's where we headed first.

The thirty-mile drive took us through thirty miles of nothing but open road and desert sand on both sides.

Then, there it was, the six-acre compound that stood like an oasis in the desert.

As we neared the front gates, I pulled out the brochure I'd picked up on the strip. "Tennis courts, swimming pool, complete gym, sports bar with a dozen TV's, two restaurants, and a minimum of forty girls on call," I said. "And there's a menu."

"For the restaurants?" Walt said.

"No."

"You mean the . . ."

"Yes. What's a Crème de Menthe French?"

"I don't know, but it sounds like something that could cost me my pension if I sampled it," Walt said.

A security guard welcomed us at the gate.

We drove to the reserved parking lot and looked around first before entering the office building connected to the main complex.

Men were lounging by the pool with beautiful young women.

Men were playing tennis with beautiful young women.

Through the bay windows of the gym, men were working out with beautiful young women.

"How much do you think it costs for this adult Disneyland?" Walt said.

"How much is in your pension fund?" I said.

"Let's go talk to Starace," Walt said.

We entered the main lobby, where a beautiful hostess greeted us with a smile.

"Welcome to the . . ." the beautiful hostess said.

Walt flashed his badge.

The beautiful hostess stopped talking.

"No trouble," Walt said. "We just want a few minutes of the owner's time."

"I don't . . . I mean . . . Carlo keeps his own . . . I'll . . ." the hostess stammered.

A very large man wearing a blue warm-up suit came out of nowhere and flanked the hostess. He had a huge head, a thick neck, and very tiny ears. Or maybe they just looked tiny compared to the bowling ball on his shoulders.

"Is there a problem?" he said.

"Only if you start one," Walt said and flashed his badge again.

Thick Neck looked at Walt's badge. "Long way from home," he said.

"The moon is a long way from home," Walt said. "This was just a three-hour plane ride."

"What do you want?" Thick Neck said.

"A few minutes of Mr. Starace's time concerning an old case I've resurrected," Walt said. "No harm, no foul. Just some talk."

Thick Neck nodded. "I'll call him."

"Any club soda or ginger ale at the bar?" Walt said. "It's hot out."

Thick Neck nodded. "I'll tell them it's comped."

While Thick Neck left the room, Walt and

I went to the bar. A half-dozen girls at the bar eyed us suspiciously. They were itching to make money, but we smelled like cop so they stayed their distance.

We drank gourmet ginger ale that was so good, I had two glasses before Thick Neck returned.

Finally, he did. "Carlo says to run you up," he said. "He's in his gym."

Run meant a golf cart trip across six acres of land, which I appreciated as it was ninety-five in the shade and I was sweating through my suit jacket.

Carlo Starace lived in a two-thousand square foot ranch home on the last acre of the compound. It had a nifty picket fence, a separate building for the gym, and a pool in the backyard.

Starace was doing bench presses when Thick Neck ushered us into the gym. A spotter stood behind the weight bench in case Starace needed help with the four hundred and five pounds he was hefting.

He didn't.

After racking the barbell, Starace sat up and looked at us. Dressed in shorts and white tank top, he was a mass of muscle and didn't mind showing it to the point of shaving his body hair.

"Long way from home," Starace said. He

stood up, took the towel offered from the spotter, and dismissed the man with a nod. "For some questions about an old case."

"Maybe so, but it's an important old case," Walt said.

"And it has what to do with me?" Starace said.

He grabbed a pair of dumbbells off a rack and started doing bicep curls with them in front of a mirror so he could watch his veins bulge.

"You were Michael Crist's chief bodyguard," Walt said.

Starace's back stiffened. He lowered the dumbbells to the rack, turned, and looked at Walt. "That was a long time ago," he said.

"Five years isn't so long ago," Walt said. "Is it?"

Starace wiped sweat from his face with a towel, tossed it aside, and said, "Let's go inside. I'll fix you guys a fruit shake with protein powder."

Inside was the kitchen.

Walt and I took seats at the chef's island while Starace prepared fruit shakes in a French-made blender.

"So, what do you want with me?" Starace said as he poured three glasses from the blender.

"This whorehouse yours?" Walt said.

"Along with two others," Starace said.

"Turn a nice profit, does it?" Walt said.

"Do I look broke?" Starace said.

Walt sipped his fruit shake. "Not bad."

"Last time I ask," Starace said. "What do you want?"

"You were Michael's bodyguard for what, thirteen years or so?"

"Yes," Starace said. "I supervised his protection here and back home."

"You traveled with him a lot?" Walt said.

"Constantly," Starace said. "The only way I could provide complete protection was to supervise hands-on. What does that have to do with your old case?"

"Thirteen years ago, I was part of a federal task force investigating Eddie Crist," I said. "I got lucky. I had an underboss as a federal witness who would have taken down Crist and Michael and a hundred others. A highly skilled assassin blew up my witness. My wife was raped and murdered in our home. My daughter, who witnessed that, is a vegetable who colors a lot."

Starace stared at me.

He sipped his fruit shake. "What does that have to do with me?" he said.

"You tell us," I said.

"Answer, nothing," Starace said. "I was just Michael's chief bodyguard, licensed and bonded by Nevada and back home. I'm a quarter Irish. Know what that means? It means I could never be a made man in the organization. It means I have no inside track to what went on at the table. All I did was keep Michael alive."

"You couldn't have been too good at your job the way things turned out," I said.

For just a second, I saw something in Starace's eyes. It was there, then it wasn't.

"Michael had quite the temper, didn't he?" I said. "When he wanted to do something, nothing stopped him. So I heard."

"The Campo family was muscling in, or trying to," Starace said. "They were original Vegas and felt they should have a bigger slice of the pie. Mr. Crist felt differently. So did Michael. Campos started disappearing at an alarming rate. They surrendered, so we thought. This place . . ."

Starace waved his hand. He had an excellent manicure.

"Was Michael's primary residence in Nevada," Starace said. "It's isolated, which makes it a destination spot, which makes it easy to see who comes and goes. It's well guarded, which made it easy to protect Michael and difficult to mount an attack against him. I didn't know, nobody knew Mike had a second place in Vegas. The

295

Campos, they knew. One night Mike sneaks out, probably to meet a broad. I thought he'd gone to sleep. The next morning, I get a call. Mike's been shot in his Vegas house. You can't protect someone who doesn't want protection. That night, Mike didn't want it. Like you said, Mike wanted to do something, nothing stopped him. After that, Mr. Crist declared all-out war and the Campos were wiped out to the last man. That's all I know. That's all I care to know."

"That's a nice story," I said. "But it has nothing to do with my witness being killed or my wife."

"No, it doesn't," Starace said. "Is that it?"

"Not quite," I said. "A highly skilled former member of the IRA was probably responsible for the bombing that killed my witness. You were with Michael round the clock back then. Did you hear anything, witness anything that suggests the possibility Michael contracted that job?"

Starace rolled his eyes.

"You don't get it, do you?" he said when he quit eye-rolling.

"Explain it to me," I said. "Simple like. I'm a simple man."

"Maybe if I was a made man I would be allowed in the room when Mike conducted business, but I wasn't," Starace said. "He could have talked to the Queen of fucking England about tea and scones, I wouldn't know about it. So is it possible, yeah, it is. Do I know anything about it, no, I don't."

"And he isn't alive to question," I said.

"No, he isn't," Starace said. "Now I'd like to get back to my workout if you don't mind and even if you do."

"One final question," I said. "How did you come to own this place?"

"What's that got to do with anything?" Starace said.

"Nothing," I said. "I'm just curious. This place must be worth millions. How does a former bodyguard buy this place from his former boss?"

Starace shrugged his massive shoulders. "Mike paid me six figures for a long time. I had very little expenses. I saved most of it. Mike and I were close friends in addition to my working for him. He knew I could never be made into the organization, but he felt I should be rewarded for my devotion. He allowed me to buy forty-nine percent from him. After he died, I purchased the remaining fifty-one percent over the past four years. It's all recorded downtown. I know as a cop, you'd like to think there's more to it than that, but there ain't. That should satisfy even a simple man like you. Anything else?"

On the return drive, Walt said, "He's slick as shit, isn't he?"

"But do you buy any of it?" I said.

"Some of it," Walt said. "He was never a made man, so it's entirely possible he knew nothing of Michael Crist's business dealings, especially contract killings."

"True," I said. "It's also true that Crist didn't start using cops as hit men until after my witness was killed, so it's entirely possibly Michael contracted Cavanaugh without his old man's knowledge. Until that time, Crist used the cops mostly as informants."

"So Michael contracted Cavanaugh, then had Cavanaugh snuffed to eliminate the one witness to his dealings," Walt said.

"It appears so."

"Can we prove any of it?"

"Not one word," I said.

I lit a smoke.

Walt concentrated on his driving.

We were silent for about ten minutes.

"You know what's bugging me?" Walt said.

"That there was an informer inside the department feeding Crist like bread to a duck?" I said.

"Yeah."

"And that informer is probably behind whoever hired the cops to kill me?"

"Yeah."

"And without that informer, my underboss would have lived to testify for a grand jury and my wife would still be alive and my daughter normal?"

"Yeah."

"Did you see a little something in Starace's eyes when I mentioned how things turned out?" I said as I lit a fresh cigarette.

"I did," Walt said. "What the fuck was that?"

"Maybe Carlo Starace is the sensitive type?" I said.

"And maybe my Aunt Mabel left me a million dollars in her will," Walt said.

"It seems the more I find out about this, the less I know," I said.

"Kind of like marriage," Walt said.

"Without the perks," I said.

"This trip isn't a total loss," Walt said. "Front row for Celine, seven-thirty tonight."

I blew smoke and looked at Walt.

He grinned. "The legs on that woman."

42

Walt and I parted company at the airport back home. Our cars were parked next to each other in long-term parking. I got into the Marquis and followed Walt's sedan to the expressway where he took the eastbound ramp and I headed for westbound.

I drove one exit, got off, and circled back to the airport. I returned my car to the lot and entered the terminal.

One hour later, I was back onboard a flight to Vegas.

Three hours after that, I checked my luggage into a locker at McCarran. I removed the Browning and stuck it down the small of my back. I rented a car. I drove straight to Starace's whorehouse from the airport.

I arrived at the front gate shortly after ten PM.

Before the guard in the shack inside the gate came out to question me, I bolted from the rental, took the gate in one jump, and hit the guard square in the chest with both feet.

The guard hit the gate, dazed and confused, but not out.

I cupped my right hand and slammed it into the soft flesh of his throat and he was finished.

I wasn't worried about surveillance cameras. Discreet was the name of the game at the Gentlemen's Escort and Sports Club. What cameras there were scanned the perimeter of the grounds and not the grounds themselves. Unless, of course, you paid extra to have yourself filmed with one of the escorts.

I dashed across six acres, staying in the shadows, and came up by Starace's back door. Only one light was on inside, stemming from the living room. He was either asleep or watching TV. I didn't peg him as much of a TV watcher and ten-thirty seemed a bit early for his night-night.

The back door was unlocked.

I went in, did a room-to-room search, then settled in on the sofa and turned off the lamp on the end table.

An hour passed.

I went to the fridge, found a two-liter plastic wide-neck bottle of ginger ale, and poured most of it down the sink.

I drank the rest of it on the sofa.

I withdrew the Browning and stuck the opening of the ginger ale bottle over the muzzle. It was a tight fit.

I used the time to review my thoughts and look for holes in my theory.

After awhile, I said fuck it and lit a smoke.

Finally, the front door opened, two figures stepped in. One of them shut the door. Even in darkness, I could make out the powerful outline of Starace. He spun the other figure around and spoke in a gruff, harsh voice.

"I've been dying for this all night," Starace rasped.

A zipper opened.

Somebody got down on their knees.

He either forgot he left a light on or didn't realize it was on when he left.

No matter.

He remembered when I clicked on the lamp.

Starace had his back against the door, pants down.

Thick Neck was on his knees with Starace's penis in his mouth.

Both men froze when the lamp came on.

"Hi, boys," I said. "First one who moves gets shot."

Starace looked at me.

"You can't do this," Starace said. "Even a

cop needs a . . ."

"Ex-cop," I said. "I never said I was still on the job. Now, Thick Neck, take his dick out of your mouth and stand up really, really slow. Understand this, I will shoot you if you so much as twitch."

Thick Neck stood up with his back to me.

"Pull up your pants," I told Starace. "You look ridiculous."

Starace yanked up his pants and looked at me.

"Now what?" he said.

"I borrowed some of your ginger ale," I said. "The plastic bottle makes a nifty homemade silencer, so if I have to shoot you no one will know until they find your very cold bodies. You, Thick Neck, walk backwards to me. Slow. I'll tell you when to stop."

Thick Neck started walking backwards.

He was counting his paces, measuring the distance between the door and the sofa.

When he was close enough, I said, "Stop," and he whirled around to make a grab for the Browning.

I smashed him just above the lip with the flat of my left hand. Like a punch in the nose, permanent damage is very little, but it stings like hell, waters the eyes, and disorients whoever is on the receiving end.

Thick Neck wobbled for a moment.

I caved in his stomach with a left hook and when he doubled over, I put him out with a crack to the back of the neck just above the spine. He would sleep for hours and awake with a migraine that would put Superman on his knees.

Carlo Starace had not moved a muscle.

"From this distance, I could put one right in the heart," I said. "Do you believe me?"

"Yes."

"Walk to me slow," I said. "Remember your friend here."

Starace walked toward me at a snail's pace. I allowed him to come within four feet of me before I waved the Browning and he stopped.

"Now talk to me," I said. "Tell me everything you know."

"I told you already, I was just a bodyguard," Starace said.

"You couldn't protect a cat from a mouse," I said. "You might ruin your manicure."

"Put the gun down and we'll see," Starace said.

"Sure."

I tossed the Browning on the sofa.

Starace stared at me in disbelief.

"All the barbells in the world won't make

you a tough guy," I said.

Starace lunged at me clumsily.

I stepped back.

He took a swing with his right fist.

I blocked it with my left arm, came in under it with my right, and drove my fist deep into his solar plexus. The blow was paralyzing.

Starace slowly sank to his knees.

I placed my right hand on Starace's forehead and guided him backward to the rug where he sucked wind.

I waited for him to recover.

I used the time to chat with him.

"You weren't Michael's bodyguard, you were his boyfriend," I said. "Isn't that right, Carlo?"

Starace sucked wind on the rug.

"That's why you traveled together back and forth from Vegas to home," I said.

Starace started to get some air back into his lungs.

"So how did it go down?" I said.

Starace looked up at me, but kept silent.

"How?" I said.

"I say anything and I'm a dead man," Starace said.

I sighed.

I placed my left foot on Starace's chest just below his neck, reached down with my right hand, and grabbed his balls.

I yanked up.

Hard.

Starace twisted like a fish out of water.

"You're going to tell me what I want to know," I said. "Or I go home with these in my pocket."

I yanked harder.

Starace sobbed in agony, helpless to do anything except cry.

I held on for several minutes until his pain was too much and Starace passed out.

I released my hold.

I went to the kitchen and found an un-opened bottle of ginger ale, poured a glass, and returned to the sofa. I sipped, sat, picked up the Browning, and waited.

After a while, Starace stirred and opened his eyes.

"Ah, there you are," I said. "Sit up, remember the gun."

It took several tries, but Starace managed to sit up.

"I'll give you one day's head start to go into hiding," I said. "Otherwise, I'll drive you to Eddie Crist's mansion in the trunk of my car. Don't be so stupid as to think I won't."

Starace nodded.

"Good. Talk."

"What do you want to know?"

"Everything," I said.

Starace nodded again.

"Mike thought the old man was losing it, getting soft," Starace said. "He didn't trust some judge or bribed jury to throw the case against him. He hired some old IRA bomber to take out your witness. Once the job was done, Mike had him killed on some island where he went to pick up his payment."

I nodded and lit a cigarette.

"My wife?" I said.

Starace watched the cigarette smoke roll up to the ceiling.

"My wife?" I said again.

"On my mother, I know nothing about that," Starace said. "Even Mike was shocked about that. He had a temper and he could be cruel, but he wasn't an animal."

"How did Michael know where my witness was being kept?" I said.

"Police informants. Mike used to joke. For pay, they say, he used to crack."

"Who?"

Starace shook his head. "Could be one or more of dozens the old man had on the payroll," he said.

I sipped ginger ale, then slowly drew on the cigarette.

"Michael dump you, is that why you killed

307

him?" I said.

"I loved him," Starace said. "I still do."

"So why'd you kill him, then?" I said.

"He was tomcatting around on me," Starace said. "He had this secret place in Vegas he thought nobody knew about, but I knew. I followed him there one night and waited for his . . . for the man he was with to leave. I went in and shot him six times. I was crazy out of my mind with jealousy. I don't even remember doing it. Eddie blamed the war with the Campos and exterminated them soon after."

I finished the ginger ale and tossed the cigarette into the glass.

"Anything else?" I said.

"If I knew who the police informers were, I would tell you," Starace said.

I stood up.

"A piece of advice," I said. "Don't go to any family members to hide. That's the first place Eddie Crist will look. Your best bet is South America. Grow a beard, drop forty pounds, and try to blend in as best you can."

Starace nodded.

I left him sitting there on his rug.

43

I was sipping morning coffee in my chair at the card table when I spotted Walt's sedan racing along the beach.

I glanced at the bag from Pat's on the card table next to my cigarettes.

I lit a smoke and watched the waves crash against the rocks. High tide was rolling in fast. Surfers in black wetsuits skimmed the waves on their boards. The sun glistened brightly on the crests.

An otherwise perfect morning.

Walt's sedan screeched to a halt and my peaceful morning came to an abrupt end.

"Jesus fucking Christ!" Walt yelled at me as he jumped out of the sedan. "Is there no goddamm end to your fucking stupidity?"

"I try never to put a limit on my talents," I said. "Want some coffee?"

"Aw, fuck," Walt said and entered the trailer. He returned a moment later with a mug and dumped himself into Oz's chair.

"You went back to Vegas," he snarled. "Why?"

I reached for the Pat's bag, removed a powdered lemon crème donut, and tossed the bag to Walt.

"Do you want to hear what I have to tell you, or do you want to scream at me all morning like the 'that's a low price' guy on TV?" I said.

Walt removed a maple walnut log from the bag. "I'm listening," he said as he bit into the log.

We ate three donuts apiece while I gave Walt the details of my second meeting with Starace.

"Son of a bitch Michael was a closet homosexual," Walt said. "But you should have told me what you were planning."

"What for?" I said. "You would have tried to stop me."

"I would have stopped you," Walt said.

"You would have tried," I said.

"If I didn't have a gut full of donut, I'd knock your head off."

I lit a cigarette and sipped from my mug.

"None of that can be used as evidence," Walt said. "Not the way you obtained it."

"Eddie Crist doesn't plan on filing a lawsuit here," I said.

Walt sighed openly.

"I think it's safe to move Janet and the boy back home with two cops round the clock for a while," I said. "I'll foot the overtime bill courtesy of my employer."

Walt nodded. "What about . . . ?"

"Carol," I said. "I believe Starace."

"So what now?" Walt said.

"Do you know where I can buy some crayons?" I said. "With the new colors."

Janet, Regan, and I ate lunch at a table in the vast backyard gardens of the Hope Springs Eternal Complex. Peanut butter, jelly, and banana sandwiches with little cartons of milk and chocolate covered Twinkies for dessert.

Father Thomas said it was Regan's favorite sandwich. She would eat it three times a day if allowed.

I ate the Twinkies before the sandwich, which drew a whisper of, "Honest to God, Jack," from Janet.

Regan ate slowly, watching the gardens as she worked her way through the sandwich, Twinkies, and milk. She showed no outward signs of enjoyment from eating, so how the priest knew it was her favorite was a mystery.

"Regan, I brought you a present," I said after she finished lunch.

Regan looked at me.

I picked up the shopping bag from the ground and set it on the table. From the bag, I removed two gift-wrapped boxes and set them in front of Regan.

Regan looked at the boxes.

"You can open them," I said.

Regan made no move toward the boxes.

"I'll help you," Janet said.

Regan shifted her eyes to Janet.

Janet slowly removed the paper from one box to reveal the carton of one hundred and twenty eight crayons, complete with built-in sharpener.

Regan looked at the crayon box.

"It's yours," I said.

Regan looked at me.

"The other one, too," Janet said.

Regan slowly reached for the second box and held it for a moment, looking at the table to avoid looking at us.

"Open it, honey," Janet said. "It's yours."

With great care not to rip the gift paper, Regan loosened the strips of tape and slowly unwrapped the deluxe set of coloring books I'd picked up at a hobby shop two towns over from mine.

Regan stared at the books, and then turned her eyes to me.

I tried hard to see something in my daughter's eyes. Some spark of life, joy, anger, something, but all I got was her dead cold stare.

"Let's pick a book," Janet suggested.

Regan opened the box and picked the first coloring book on top. It was a map of the fifty states. Colors were selected for topography. Green for plains, brown for mountains, blue for rivers, and so on.

Regan studied the first page. Alabama. She selected the crayons she would need, removed them from the box, and got right to work.

She didn't look at us again.

In her mind, we were dismissed.

I sat behind the wheel of the Marquis.

Janet sat beside me.

We didn't speak.

I started to cry.

It started slowly at first.

I didn't even realize the tears were flowing.

I saw my hands shake on the steering wheel.

"Jack?" Janet said, softly.

I tried hard to suck it in.

"Let it go, Jack," Janet said. "Just let it go."

What came out was uncontrolled raw

emotion. I sat and cried, sobbed so hard I couldn't breathe. No matter how hard I tried to regain control, I couldn't stop the river of tears running down my face.

Janet put her arm around me.

I should have been embarrassed to show such weakness in front of Janet, but I wasn't.

"Just let it all out, Jack," Janet said. "For once and for all, let it all out, then let go."

I did.

My eyes finally went dry. The sobbing stopped. My breathing came under control. I got out of the Marquis and lit a cigarette.

Janet came out of her door, walked around, and stood beside me.

"That was the worst of it," she said.

I nodded.

"You can't help being who you are, Jack," Janet said.

I looked at her.

"Who am I?"

"A very tough man with a heart no stronger that warm Jell-O," Janet said. "You'll just have to deal with that."

"It was easier to deal with when I was drinking," I said.

Janet gave me her eyes.

"You can't drink anymore and be my man," she said.

"Is that what I am," I said.

"You'll just have to deal with that, too," Janet said.

I tossed the cigarette and reached for the car door.

"While you were relieving some tension, I had a thought," Janet said. "Two, actually. The first is that we go back to your junk-yard and I make love to you until your gums bleed."

"How does that work?"

"You'll just have to find out."

"The second?"

"I'm curious as to what Regan would do if we went back in and colored with her," Janet said.

I looked at her.

"Nothing ventured," Janet said.

We returned to the garden where Regan was on page three. She didn't look up from the page when we sat down opposite her.

Janet grabbed two coloring books and some crayons.

"I'm not very good at this, I'm afraid," Janet said.

We colored.

Janet's page was a mess.

Mine was a disaster.

Regan put down her crayons and looked at our pages. She didn't speak, but she came around to our side and sat between us.

Regan sighed, picked up a crayon, and showed us how it was done.

After her demonstration, Regan looked at Janet, then at me as if to say, *Got that?*

Then, just as silently, Regan returned to her spot and continued her masterpiece.

I thought, for just a fleeting second, I saw a smile cross Regan's lips.

44

"My son was a homosexual," Crist said.

His voice was heavy, filled with his own impending death. I had been talking for more than an hour and those were his first words when I concluded.

"And responsible for my witness, but not my wife," I said. "There's a third party in the mix."

"How can you be sure this Starace was telling the truth?" Crist said.

"He has a glass heart to match his glass head," I said. "Besides, the details were too precise. No rapid eye movement, looking left or right, blinking, or indications of dishonesty."

Crist allowed a tiny smile to cross his lips. "That's right, you're trained for that kind of thing," he said.

"I was trained to uphold the law," I said.

"And now you've broken it," Crist said. "And like a virgin on her wedding night, it's one thing that can't be fixed once it's busted."

We were under the awning with glasses of iced tea.

At the pool, Campbell Crist tanned in a recliner.

"I made some calls to the airport this morning," I said. "Starace got on a plane to Brazil one way."

"Not too bright, is he?" Crist said.

"No."

"He has to answer for my son."

"I know."

"Who answers for your wife?"

"I don't know," I said. "An informer inside the department, probably. Somebody with a great deal to lose if my case went to grand jury and names were named. Somebody Michael had on his payroll that was stupid enough to panic and stick his head above ground."

"You took the long road around to say it was a cop," Crist said.

"Yes."

"So your job isn't complete yet."

"No."

Crist looked past me to Campbell. She had turned over onto her stomach.

"The way it works, the way to recruit cops or a judge onto the payroll, is to selectively find the weak in need," Crist said. "Weak doesn't necessarily mean they can be bribed. Neither does in need. Together is a winning combination. In a crisis, the weak will panic. Panic will make a man do just about anything."

I heard a noise and looked at Campbell. She was sitting up, removing her top. She tossed it on the table next to the recliner and picked up a bottle of suntan lotion.

"Is it possible your son had a separate list of informers from yours?" I said.

"Not possible, highly likely," Crist said. "It may have even overlapped. I don't know and I have no way of verifying so many years after the fact."

"Those still active, do you have a list?" I said.

"Somebody who took money from me or my son murdered your wife," Crist said. "I started this with you to find that person for my own selfish reasons. Those reasons haven't changed."

"I won't share names with the authorities," I said. "My word on that."

Crist looked at me.

"My doctors say I have weeks, maybe a month at best," he said. "Do you think I really care at this stage if some judge gets what's coming to him?"

Campbell stood up and dove into the pool. Crist shook his head.

"Modesty is a lost art," he said. "I'll call Clark this afternoon. Go by tomorrow morning. He'll have something for you."

I nodded and was about to stand up.

"If you find him while I'm still alive, do not kill him," Crist said. "That's my pleasure. It won't get me into heaven, but it will make hell a lot more palatable."

"For the both of us," I said. "What if I find him after?"

"I'm dead?"

I nodded.

"Then kill him in the name of vengeance," Crist said. "If anybody understands that, it's the man upstairs. After all, he said it first."

45

Oz was wearing some snappy-looking new clothes when he came walking down the beach to my trailer. Tan slacks, peach-colored Polo shirt, white shoes, and a nifty-looking straw hat for the sun.

"Going on three weeks without a drink," he said when he arrived. "I never thought I'd make that long."

"Want some coffee?" I said.

"I do."

I went into my trailer for the fresh pot I'd set to brew and returned with it and two mugs. I filled the mugs and gave one to Oz.

We sipped.

I fired up a smoke.

Oz scratched his scraggly beard.

"Did you know the first two nights in that house, your sister-in-law slept in a chair in my room?" Oz said. "Helped me through the cold sweats and the shakes. Fed me soup and kept me clean when I peed my pants."

I didn't know, but it didn't surprise me, either.

We sipped.

I smoked.

"I got rid of all booze in my trailer," Oz said. "Poured it down the sink last night when I got home. Figured it's hard enough without temptation staring me in the face."

"Feel like going to breakfast?" I said.

"What, you mean to town?"

"Why not? The diner serves a decent omelet and why shouldn't two old friends go to breakfast once in a while?"

"You want to walk or take your car?" Oz said.

"Walk," I said. "Definitely walk."

"Let me put on my walking shoes and get my wallet."

"Get the shoes, leave the wallet," I said.

Picking up a tail in a car is not so difficult if you suspect you're being followed. Look for the car three lengths back that stays with you for an extended period of time and ninety-nine times out of a hundred that's your guy. If on a highway, get off and drive side streets and if he's still with you, it's for a reason.

Marking a tail on foot is much more difficult. Whoever is tailing you has surely made the effort to blend in with the environment and present him- or herself as part of the scenery. In a mall, carry shopping bags. On the street, a newspaper works. The trick is to become invisible.

The late morning sun was hot. Dozens of surfers bounced around like corks in the water. Sunbathers on towels filled the sand. A group played Frisbee. Another group tossed a foam football. A man walked his dog. A woman walked her dog. In other words, the beach area was crowded.

One way to pick out a tail on foot is to see who is taking great care not to notice you as you walk by. Spying while you read the paper and not getting caught doing it is an art form few have perfected.

I took mental notes as Oz and I walked at a leisurely pace to town.

Woman walking dog didn't break stride.

Man reading book didn't do the casual glance.

Man walking dog looked, but didn't care.

Man with radio did the casual turnover as we walked by.

Man with radio propped himself up on his elbows for a better view.

Man with radio was the likely tail.

We reached the edge of town where a small municipal lot abutted the entrance to the beach. I counted seven parked cars, two minivans and one pickup. The vans and truck were too easy to spot on the road. Four of the cars were red and they stood out like fireballs from the sky. Two of the remaining cars were sports cars, useless for surveillance. Too low to the ground to watch the streets. The seventh car was a gray sedan with nothing to distinguish it from the crowd.

It was exactly the kind of car I would use.

Oz and I took a booth by the window that gave me a clear view to the parking lot.

We ordered omelets, home fries, grilled English muffins, juice, and coffee. I lathered my muffins in blueberry jam. Oz went with strawberry. Either way, you couldn't go wrong.

I was nearly done with my omelet when I spotted Radioman entering the parking lot. He was now wearing blue jeans and a tee shirt and carried the radio in his left hand. He went to the gray sedan, opened the door with a key, and got in behind the wheel.

"I could use a couple more English muffins," I said to Oz.

"Thinking the same thing," Oz said. "Amazing how much better food tastes when your tongue isn't clogged with booze."

Radioman stayed put behind the wheel of

the gray sedan.

We ate second helpings of muffins with coffee, lingered over the coffee, and finally had our fill. I paid the check and kept a casual eye on Radioman as we strolled back to the beach.

I paused at the sand to fire up a smoke, turning my back against the slight breeze, a move that allowed me to glance Radioman's way. He was adjusting the outside mirror to keep an eye on me.

With our stomachs full, our stroll home would have embarrassed a snail. Forty minutes for a twenty-minute walk.

It was deliberate on my part.

Nothing stews inexperienced operatives in their own juices like having to wait for the next move. When the wait is overly long, carelessness usually follows.

Finally, Oz and I neared his trailer.

"I was thinking I should stop by and thank your brother for my license," I said.

Oz looked at me.

I stole a glance backward.

Radioman was strolling near the water.

"What you mean is I should get off my ass and go visit Albert," Oz said.

"That's what I mean and I'll even drive you, but right now I think I'd like to use your bedroom window," I said.

Oz looked at me with the expression usually reserved for foreign languages spoken at you when all you speak is English.

"I'm being watched," I said. "I want to find out why."

"I should ask no questions, huh?"

"No."

Oz dug out his key, unlocked the door, and opened it.

We entered his trailer normally and Oz closed the door.

I immediately went to the window and peered through his sheer summer curtains. I noticed Oz had done a great deal of tidying up once back home. The place looked cheery.

"Place looks good, Oz," I remarked.

"Thank you," Oz said.

Radioman was headed toward the beach. He paused at a position that allowed him a view of Oz's trailer, removed his shirt and pants, and casually spread out with his back to the water.

Oz stood next to me and peeked through the curtains. "Who?"

"Man with the radio," I said.

"What if . . ."

"You're not his target," I said.

"Shouldn't we call the cops?" Oz said.

"No. Now listen, I want you to wait until

I go out the window," I said. "Then I want you to go outside, leave the door open, and putz around with something, but make off like you're talking to me still inside. Got that?"

"Yeah."

I turned away from the window.

"Hey, John," Oz said. "This is kind of exciting."

"Keep watching, it might get better."

I entered Oz's bedroom, opened the window as wide as it would go, wiggled out, and hit the sand. I stayed low until I heard the door open and Oz step out.

"Rinse that out good while I check for the leak," Oz said, loud enough to be heard by Radioman.

I walked away from the trailer until I was below Radioman's line of sight, then veered right and walked to my own trailer. I paused to pick up Radioman. He was focused on Oz while he fiddled with a radio knob and did his best to appear casual.

I walked about a hundred yards down the beach, cut right, and walked to the water. Tide was low. The wet sand stretched out an extra hundred yards. I skimmed the water's edge and came up directly behind Radioman.

He was stretched out now, faking sleep

with his head on his arms so he could keep watch on Oz. When I knelt down beside the radio, his back stiffened.

"Don't move, don't twitch, and certainly don't make any attempt to get up," I said. "I have a Browning Hi-power, but I won't need it for the likes of you. Nod if you understand."

Radioman nodded.

"Good," I said. "You want to hear a joke? An old one, kind of sexist, but appropriate under the circumstances."

"What?" Radioman said.

"My joke," I said. "Do you want to hear it?"

"Sure."

"What did the dumb blonde say after sex?" I said.

"What?"

I nudged Radioman with my elbow. "What did the dumb blonde say after sex?"

"I don't know, man. What does that . . . ?"

"Which team are you on," I said.

"I don't . . . oh, I get it. What does that . . . ?"

I stood up and nudged Radioman with my foot. "Translation, who are you, what team do you play for?"

"I have ID," Radioman said. "In my pants,

my wallet."

"Glad to hear it," I said. "Get up."

Radioman slowly stood up.

"Don't turn around," I said. "See that old man there at his trailer?"

"The black guy?"

"Yeah. Pick up your pants, shirt, and radio and walk straight to him. I'll be right behind you and remember the Browning," I said. "I just had a nice breakfast and I'm in no mood for running, so I'll just shoot you in the leg if you rabbit. Move."

Radioman started walking.

I stayed a foot or so behind him.

As we neared Oz, he stopped puttering and looked at us.

"Who's this fool?" Oz said as we arrived.

"That's what I'm going to find out," I said. "Right now."

"I don't want any trouble," Radioman said.

Oz had three beach chairs at a round table in front of his trailer.

"Sit," I told Radioman.

He sat. Up close, I could see he was young, still in his twenties. His blue eyes were filled with fear and uncertainty.

"All I'm . . ." Radioman said.

I held up my right hand.

"You don't talk," I said.

329

Radioman looked at me.

"Your wallet," I said.

Radioman dug his wallet out from his pants and held it out to me.

"Toss it," I said.

He tossed. I caught. I opened it and looked at the driver's license.

"This your real name?" I said.

Radioman nodded. "Who'd make up a name like that?"

"What?" Oz said.

"Ernest Horacio," I said. "Ferrer."

"What kinda fucking name is that?" Oz said.

"My mother is English. My father is from Spain. They met on the bullet train on the way to . . ." Radioman said.

"Oh, shut up," I said.

I flipped through the wallet. I removed an ID that said Ernest worked as a security guard at the County Mall.

"This where you work?" I said.

"Yeah, but it's just temporary. I'm on the waiting list for the state police. I should be called in two years or less."

"I'm sure the state police and the mall are popping their buttons over you," I said.

"I scored in the top five percent on the state police exam," Ernest said.

"You believe this kid," I said to Oz.

"I love him," Oz said.

"Why you tailing me, Ernie?" I said.

"I'm not supposed to say," Ernest said.

Oz rolled his eyes.

"Really?" I said. "No kidding."

"Were you dropped on your head as a baby or something?" Oz said.

"Ernie, you're about one second away from a pistol whipping," I said.

I pulled the Browning from the small of my back and held it loosely in my right hand for Ernie to see.

"That's illegal," Ernest said.

"Was that a question on the state police exam?" I said.

I turned to Oz.

"Get some rope," I said. "We're going to tie this idiot to your kitchen chair inside. Then I'm going to cut his fingers and toes off with garden shears. If that doesn't work, I'll take his dick."

Ernest went a little green in the face.

"You're just saying that to scare me," he said.

"Really?" I said. "Okay, let's try this."

I shoved the Browning down my pants, grabbed Ernest by the hair, and yanked him forward from the chair. He hit the sand face first, where I dragged him three feet by his hair before I let him go and stuck my right foot on the back of his neck.

"All I have to do is step down and if you live, you'll never walk again," I said. "If you don't live, it's a moot point."

"Please," Ernest sobbed. "I have to go pee-pee."

I froze.

Oz looked at me.

"What did you say?" I said.

"I have to make pee-pee," Ernest sobbed.

I removed my foot, walked to a chair, and sat.

"Get up," I told Ernest.

Slowly Ernest stood.

"Sit down next to me," I said.

Ernest took the chair opposite me at the table.

"Oz, you got anything cold to drink?" I said.

"Got some cans of ginger ale on ice," Oz said and went inside.

"That will do," I said.

I lit a smoke and looked at Ernest.

"Wipe your nose and tell me why you're tailing me," I said.

Oz returned with three cold cans of ginger ale. We popped the lids and took sips.

"G'head," I told Ernest.

"I was on duty at the mall when . . ."

"When?" I said.

"When, what?"

"My God, he's stupid," Oz said.

"Were you on duty at the mall?" I said.

"Oh," Ernest said. "Three nights ago. I work four to midnight. The mall closes at eleven. Anyway, I was in the office doing the nightly paperwork when this man walks into the office and shows me a state police badge. He said he was conducting background surveillance on a subject and needed a few guys nobody knew to help him. He said he saw my test scores and would guarantee I'd be moved up the list if I agreed to help him. He also paid me two hundred and fifty dollars a day, plus expenses. All I had to do was follow you around for a few days and report back to him what I saw. He had your address and a photograph of you from some old newspaper story."

"What did he look like?" I said.

"Tall, well built. Had blond hair, but I couldn't tell how long because he wore a hat. He had . . ."

"What kind of hat?" I said.

"The hat?"

"Yes, the hat. What kind of hat was it?"

"Like the hat Indiana Jones wore, like that."

"A fedora."

"I guess."

"What else?"

"He had a mustache," Ernest said. "A big, bushy one like a walrus."

"Glasses, scars, anything like that?"

"Sunglasses," Ernest said. "Aviator sunglasses."

"At night?"

Ernest nodded.

"His name on the ID, what was it?"

"James Wight," Ernest said.

"Age?"

"Old," Ernest said. "About your age."

In the background, Oz snorted a laugh.

"You think I'm old?" I said.

"Well," Ernest said.

"You'll get there," I said. "Maybe."

Ernest sipped his ginger ale.

"How were you supposed to report to him?"

"He said in three nights, he'd return for my written reports," Ernest said. "He paid me in advance. Seven hundred and fifty dollars."

"He would just show up?" I said.

Ernest nodded.

I thought a moment, sipped ginger ale, and lit a fresh smoke.

"You said a couple of guys," I said. "Who else did he hire?"

"I don't know," Ernest said. "He gave me a cell phone number to call if you left your trailer on foot. I assume the other guy was to follow you if you took your car."

"So I walked to town for breakfast and you called the cell number?" I said.

Ernest nodded. "I followed you to see where you went, but I'm not supposed to tail you by car. That's the other guy's job."

I thought, sipped, smoked.

"All I wanted to do was get ahead on the waiting list," Ernest said.

"Shut up," I said.

Oz took a seat next to me.

I slowly put it all together.

"Come on," I said and stood up.

The three of us walked down to my trailer where the Marquis was parked beside the card table.

I popped the hood.

We looked at the C-4 plastic explosives wired to the ignition system.

"Is that a bomb?" Ernest said.

"It ain't a cake warmer, kid," Oz said.

I pulled out my cell phone and called Walt.

"Bring the SWAT Bomb Squad over to my place," I told Walt.

"Why?" Walt said.

"I just bought the Marquis and I really like it," I said and hung up.

46

From the safety of Oz's table, I watched the four-man SWAT team disassemble the bomb under the hood of my car. To do this job, work on the bomb squad that is, requires certain characteristics not found in the average person. Highly specialized training, for one. Nerves of steel, coupled with the ability to maintain cool composure under tremendous stress, the willingness to do the job and super-sized balls made of pure high-octane lead.

Oz sat to my left.

Walt sat to my right.

Ernest sat in the back of Walt's sedan.

I sipped coffee and lit a smoke.

Walt said, "It's absolutely impossible for any human being to be as stupid as that kid. Just not possible."

"He's on the waiting list for the state cops," I said.

"God forbid," Walt said.

"Somebody sure wants you dead," Oz said, looking at me.

"Seems that way," I said.

"No more fucking around, John," Walt said. "Time to move out of this shithole and go into protective custody."

"Until when?" I said. "The Po-leece solve the twelve-year-old murder of my wife?"

"That isn't fair, John," Walt said.

"Maybe not, but tell me I'm wrong."

"Hey, Lieutenant!" a SWAT officer yelled.

We looked.

He waved us over.

"Oz, you stay here," I said.

"No shit, I'll stay here," Oz said.

Walt and I walked to the Marquis.

The SWAT team leader held up the block of C-4.

"No detonator charge," he said.

Walt looked at me.

"I don't get it," Walt said. "Why bother to wire C-4 if you don't intend to blow up what you wire?"

The SWAT team leader held up a small slip of paper.

"Taped to the underside of the C-4," he said.

I took the paper and read the typed note. *The next one will go off and you won't be able to protect her.*

The paper fell from my hand.

For a moment, I was still.

With keys in hand, I turned and raced to the Marquis.

Walt picked up the paper.

"Stop him!" Walt yelled.

The SWAT team leader grabbed my left shoulder. I spun left and smashed his nose with the heel of my right hand.

Blood squirted.

"Jesus Christ!" he yelled.

Two other SWAT officers grabbed me. I dropped one with a kick to the knee and spun the other into the hood of the Marquis. The fourth jumped me from behind and pinned my arms.

"Cuff him, cuff him," Walt said.

I smashed the back of my head into the face of SWAT officer holding my arms and he let me go. I swept him at the knee and he dropped.

I moved to the Marquis and Walt hit me from behind with something really hard.

I opened my eyes in the back seat of Walt's sedan next to Ernest. My wrists were cuffed to the iron ring built into the front seat. The door was open. Walt and Oz were drinking ginger ale at my card table.

"They've had three glasses already,"

Ernest said, when he saw I was awake.

"Walt, get these fucking things off me or so help me God, I'll tear your fucking seat apart," I said. "I'll use my goddamn teeth if I have to."

Walt stood up and walked to the open car door. He sipped ginger ale from his glass before speaking.

"Six of my detectives have taken Regan to the safe house, along with her doctor and for some reason, a nun," Walt said.

"Thank you," I said.

"Your little Wild West show back there put four men in the emergency room," Walt said. "One broken nose. One dislocated shoulder. One busted kneecap. One broken face. Next time, before you . . ."

"What's a broken face?" Ernest said.

"You shut up," Walt said. "Or I'll show you."

"Get these off me," I said.

"I'm going with you," Walt said.

"What about me?" Ernest said. "I still have to pee."

"You . . . you're under house arrest until I get back," Walt said. "You'll stay here with Oz. If you're not here when I return, I'll burn the fucking mall down with you in it."

Walt set me free, then Ernest.

I got out and Walt yanked Ernest to his feet.

"Remember what I told you," Walt said.

Ernest nodded, then looked at Oz. "Got anything to eat around here?"

Oz rolled his eyes.

"Where's your bathroom, man," Ernest said.

"That pretty much confirms what we thought," Walt said. "A snitch, informer, inside man to Crist, whatever the fuck you want to call him has been dormant all these years until you woke up and spilled his apples."

I looked at Walt.

"You mean rocked the apple cart?"

"Some fucking thing with apples," Walt said. "Point is, I swear on my life I won't let anything happen to Regan. I give you my word as your friend, your ex-partner, and whatever else you want my word on."

"I know that already, Walt."

"I know you know, but I want you to give me your word you won't go off and kill somebody in the first degree," Walt said. "The investigation is live now and we'll spare no manpower to find this asshole and bring him in. Your word, John?"

"That I won't commit murder or that I'll

stop my investigation?" I said.

"I know you won't stop, so I'll settle for murder," Walt said. "I'd hate to have to put the bracelets on you for real, but you know that I will."

"I'd expect no less from you," I said.

"Good," Walt said.

"What did you hit me with?" I said.

"Handle of my retractable baton," Walt said. "You just ripped the shit out of four SWAT, what did you think I was going to use, my shoe?"

My cell phone rang.

"Mr. Bekker, Mr. Clark calling," Clark said when I answered the call. "I was expecting you to stop by my office today."

"I'll have to put that off until tomorrow, Mr. Clark," I said. "Somebody planted a bomb in my car today and threatened my daughter. I'm with the police right now."

"Were you injured?" Clark said.

"No, but I have to see to my daughter."

"By all means," Clark said. "Call me tomorrow if possible."

"I will. Thanks."

I put the cell phone away and lit a smoke.

"Who was that?" Walt said.

"Clark of Lewis and Clark."

"The mob lawyer?"

I nodded.

"And?"

"And nothing," I said. "I was to see him today for Crist. I didn't keep the appointment."

"What I said about murder goes for withholding evidence or information," Walt said. "Lawyers or otherwise."

"Sure," I said. "Now can we please get to my daughter? I can run faster backwards than you're driving."

47

Regan was wearing a bicycle helmet when Walt and I arrived at the safe house. Six of Walt's detectives stood around her and watched as my daughter, in a complete freak out, smashed her head against the wall. She smashed and banged, spun and kicked over a lamp, got on her knees and banged her helmet against the rug. Father Thomas and Sister Mary Martin allowed Regan to pound the helmet and silently scream, until finally, Regan slumped to the floor and cried noiseless tears in her hands.

Exhausted, Regan closed her eyes and fell into a deep sleep.

There was nothing any of us could do but watch.

Thomas asked me to carry Regan to the sofa and I gently lifted her from the floor and lowered her to the softer cushions. Thomas removed the helmet. Every few seconds, Regan twitched.

I looked at the priest.

"Nothing to worry about," Thomas said.

He fixed a sedative and injected Regan with it. Moments later, she went from deep but restless sleep to a more relaxed state of unconsciousness.

"She'll be all right," Thomas said. "She doesn't like change. She doesn't like anything to break up her routine. She needs the necessity of the expected."

"It may be necessary to keep her here for awhile," I said.

"How long?" Thomas said.

"We don't know," I said.

"This could be a major setback for her," Sister Mary Martin said.

"Worse than being kidnapped or murdered?" I said.

"Who would want to harm this child?" Sister Mary Martin said.

"The same person or persons who murdered my wife and caused Regan to be like this in the first place," I said.

Sister Mary Martin's normally composed face slowly morphed into a mask of anger. Her lips became tight lines, her brows furrowed, her nose flared. "I would protect this child with my life," the nun rasped. "And if I have to, I would take a life to protect hers."

"Now, Sister," Thomas said.

"Oh, to hell with that, Father," Sister Mary Martin snapped at the priest. "I've spent ten years with this child and I'll not allow some murderous son of a bitch to harm her because he's afraid of prison."

"Sister, take it easy," I said. "This place is called a safe house. That means . . ."

"I've been to the movies, Mr. Bekker," the nun said to me. "I know what a safe house is. I assume these officers will be staying with us until that no good bastard is apprehended?"

"Yes," I said.

"Good. Which bedroom is hers?" Sister Mary Martin said.

"Pick one."

The nun walked down the hall to the bedrooms to check them out.

I looked at Thomas.

"She's no one to fool with, is she?" I said.

"An Irish Catholic nun is a force to be reckoned with," Thomas said.

Sister Mary Martin returned. She brought her force with her.

"The first bedroom on the left will do nicely," the nun told Thomas.

Thomas turned to me. "Would you carry her to her room?"

I gently lifted Regan off the sofa. She weighed no more than a hundred and five or ten pounds at best. I carried her into the bedroom with Thomas and the nun behind me. The bed was already turned down.

"Now leave us, please," Sister Mary Martin said.

Thomas and I returned to the living room where Walt was giving last-minute instructions to his six detectives.

I said goodnight to Thomas and walked outside for some fresh air and a smoke. For the moment, my anger was gone, pushed to the back burner by the need for rational, clear-headed thinking.

Anger is a weakness that clouds your mind and judgment. Cops are trained to step outside the situation, divorce their emotions from rational thinking and work analytically.

Try doing that when your daughter is beating her head against a wall.

As I was stepping on the spent butt of the cigarette, Walt came and joined me. His face was gray, ashen, his eyes filled with a strange emotion.

"I didn't . . . I mean, I had no idea how . . . aw, hell, John, I don't know what to say," Walt stammered.

"Say nothing," I said. "Just do me a favor and give me a ride to Janet's house."

Walt nodded.

Silently, we walked to his sedan.

Silently, Walt drove while I smoked.

An hour or so later, as we arrived in Janet's driveway, Walt spoke for the first time since we'd entered the car.

"John, I want you to know nothing will be spared until we find this guy," Walt said. "Detectives, manpower, overtime, I'm using it all. Even Lawrence at the FBI."

"I know that," I said.

Walt nodded. He didn't look at me.

"Don't do anything that could cost you, John," Walt said. "I'm your friend. Crist is not. Try to remember that, okay?"

"Call me if something breaks," I said and got out.

I walked to the door and rang the bell.

Walt backed out of the driveway and drove away.

Janet answered the door.

"Don't say anything," I said. "Just let me sleep on the sofa, because if you don't, I'm going to get blind stinking drunk tonight."

48

We ate a quiet dinner as a little family.

I couldn't tell you what the meal consisted of as it all blended together in a tasteless dish that went down like boiled rubber.

Mark sensed something wasn't right and he kept quiet, minded Janet when she told him to clean his plate, and didn't complain when she told him to rinse and stack the dishes in the dishwasher.

When Janet told Mark that we had adult business to discuss, the boy didn't make a fuss when she sent him to his room.

Janet brewed a pot of coffee.

"Let's have our coffee outside," Janet said.

It was dark by the time we sat outside at the patio table and drank our coffee.

I lit a cigarette.

Janet didn't say anything about it and trotted out an old, tin ashtray from the kitchen somewhere.

"Now why are you thinking of drinking

again, Jack?" Janet said, quietly.

I told her.

"I don't know if I should give you a hug or slap your face again," Janet said.

"I could use the hug," I said. "Why a slap?"

"At a time when your child needs your help, understanding, and protection, you want to crawl back inside a bottle," Janet said. "I hardly think that kind of cowardice deserves a hug, do you?"

"No."

"I'm glad that you turned to me, though," Janet said.

"No choice," I admitted. "I don't think there is anybody else who could stop me."

"Because you love me and don't want to lose me?" Janet said.

I thought about that for a moment.

"Yes," I said.

"You don't have to sleep on the sofa," Janet said.

"It will help me focus on what I have to do," I said.

"Should I ask what that is?"

"No."

49

David Clark saw me midmorning the following day. After leaving Janet's, I drove home to shave, shower and change into my one good suit before driving to Clark's office suite.

We met in the conference room. Coffee, juice, and water were in place on the table.

I took the coffee.

"Mr. Crist has assured me that the names on this list will never be made public or used in any way that could be construed as part of a criminal investigation," Clark said.

"Yes," I said.

"However, Mr. Crist will shortly not be among us anymore," Clark said.

I read between the lines.

"You want assurances I will keep my word once Crist is gone," I said.

"I do."

"What would you like?" I said.

"The question isn't what I would like, but

what you will agree to," Clark said.

"Which is?"

"I have two lists," Clark said. "The actual list of names and a second list where your name has been added as an informer for the Crist family. It contains information on you such as how long you've been an informer, how much money you took, and where it's hidden. If one word of the actual list surfaces, the second list goes to the FBI. My way of assuring that you'll keep your word."

"I could prove that to be false," I said.

"Oh, I don't think you could," Clark said. "And even if you could, you'd require millions of dollars to defend yourself and I don't think you have that."

"I'll agree," I said. "But not because of your threats, Mr. Clark. Because I gave my word that I would."

"Nonetheless."

"Let me see the list."

Alone in the conference room, I read the list, the one without my name on it. I was astounded at the names of people sworn to uphold the law who broke their vow by taking bribe money from the Crist organization.

Federal, state, and local judges.

Federal, state, and local prosecutors.

Police chiefs around the country.

Deputy chiefs.

Captains, lieutenants, and detectives.

State police chiefs.

State police detectives and investigators.

County clerks.

Federal licensing agents.

IRS agents and supervisors.

Businesses around the country, including big oil and gaming.

High-ranking mob members from Italy, Sicily, Russia, China, and all poppy producing countries.

Members of Congress and the Senate.

The list overlapped with Michael Crist's secondary list.

Michael's list was more localized to Vegas and home.

Officers of major companies.

Wall Street brokers.

Cops of any and all ranks.

Members of City Hall in Vegas and home.

Zoning committees.

The list went back three decades.

Many on the list had passed away or retired. As those retired or died, new names took their place. They weren't paid as well. They had to earn their stripes before the big money flowed.

One name occupied both lists.

It was all I had to go on.

It was enough.

Clark was putting on a portable green in his office when I barged in without knocking.

Clark sank a fifteen-foot putt into the metal hole.

"Finished?" he said as he set the putter aside.

"Yes."

I set the lists on Clark's desk.

"Good."

"Question," I said. "How much did it cost to have all those tests on Michael and his people fudged?"

Clark stared at me.

I grabbed Clark by his two-hundred dollar tie and pulled it so tight it cut into his neck like piano wire.

"I can't . . ." Clark rasped.

"I'll keep my word because I gave it," I said. "But, if you think a sniveling little piece of crap like you can threaten me, think twice. If you ever mention my name to anybody, call me up, send me a letter, nod if you see me on the street, I will fucking kill you. That's it."

I released the tie with a shove. Clark hit his desk and fell to his eighty-dollar-a-square-foot rug.

"Any questions?" I said.

Clark struggled to loosen the tie, looked at me, and shook his head.

I didn't close the door on the way out.

50

Janet was just about ready to leave for her twelve-hour shift at the hospital when I rang her doorbell.

"I'd like to see if Mark would like to go to the park and shag some fly balls," I said.

"Are you kidding?" Janet said. "He'd love to, but I'm off to work and the sitter will be here any moment."

"How much does the sitter get?"

"Forty bucks for thirteen hours."

I removed two twenties and a ten from my fold. "Give her this," I said. "Tell her the extra ten is for the inconvenience."

"What about dinner and his bedtime?"

"Got it covered," I said. "Go to work."

Janet gave me that look only a woman can express when she wants to believe you, but isn't quite sure.

"No pizza. No soda. Nine-thirty bedtime tops," Janet said.

"Absolutely."

We took turns hitting fungos on the baseball field at the local park. I showed Mark how to judge fly balls from the outfield and he caught several dozen before we made the switch.

Then I hit ground balls around the infield and showed him how to move to his right and left for shortstop and second base, the way to pivot for a double play ball. Third was to the left, back, and directly ahead type of position, requiring a different sort of throw to first than the other two infield positions.

I showed him how to field off the mound, to cover first on a bunt and third on a squeeze play when a runner was on second. I showed him how to cover home plate on a passed ball or wild pitch and how to back up the catcher.

We quit around six.

I thought the boy exhausted.

He wasn't.

We arrived home and when I asked about his dinner preference, Mark licked his lips and inquired about pizza.

I ordered two with sausage and extra cheese, garlic rolls, and, to wash it down with, a two-liter bottle of ginger ale.

We watched a ball game while we ate.

The Seattle Mariners beat the Los Angeles Dodgers in an interleague game three to one. The Mariners scored two runs in the top of the ninth inning. In a nail biter, the Dodgers loaded the bases with no outs in the bottom of the ninth and failed to score after a strikeout and a double play ended the game.

It was ten-thirty.

"What time does your mom usually get home?" I said.

"I think one," Mark said. "Sometimes I wake up when she gets in and is talking to Susan, my sitter."

"Oh, boy," I said. "You best get to bed while I try to hide the pizza boxes and clean up a bit."

"You're not afraid of my mom?" Mark said, skeptically.

"You bet," I said.

"She's a girl."

"That's why. Go."

I was watching a very young Cary Grant try to evade the charms of a very young Kate Hepburn in a very old movie when I fell asleep on the sofa.

I woke up when Janet came walking in from the kitchen.

She had come in through the back door,

stopping first at the trash bins to retrieve the folded pizza boxes I'd tried to hide under some plastic bags.

"You're way too smart for me," I said.

"Never forget that," Janet said. "I'm going to soak in a hot tub after I check on Mark. If you would care to join me in a bubble bath extravaganza, that would be lovely."

It was just that.

Lovely.

Bubbles and all.

51

Breakfast was taken at the backyard patio table where Mark snuck scraps of bacon to Molly.

"If you had ideas of keeping that cat, I'd forget them," Janet said when Mark took Molly to the end of the yard to play. "Unless you had the notion of moving in here with us."

I sipped coffee and looked at Janet over the rim of the cup.

"Okay, too much too fast," Janet said.

Molly snared a butterfly and Mark chased her to try to save the delicate creature.

"Yesterday might have been the best day of his life," Janet said as she watched Mark grab Molly and free the butterfly. "I thank you for that."

"If we're going to have a serious relationship, you would want and require complete honesty from me," I said.

"Both ways," Janet said.

I watched Mark and Molly for a moment. If not for certain events in my life, Regan might be his babysitter and Janet my Thanksgiving dinner fantasy.

"You're going to say something I'm not going to like, aren't you," Janet said.

I looked at her.

She lowered her eyes.

"When I leave here, I'm driving directly to the man who murdered Carol and banished Regan to a mental institution for probably the rest of her life," I said. "And I'm going to kill him."

Janet kept her eyes on the table.

"That's it," I said.

"I won't attempt to stop you and I won't tell the police," Janet said. "I know that you're going to do what you have to because you are who you are."

Janet's eyes slowly rose and she looked at me with quiet dignity and determination.

"But if you deliberately commit cold-blooded murder, never return to my home," she said.

I stood up from the table and walked away.

Janet's eyes were hot on my back.

52

The average bed and breakfast is empty of guests by eleven in the morning. Most who stay at B&B's want to save on expensive hotel bills and get a free breakfast. After they eat, they are out and on their way to business meetings, sightseeing, wherever.

I arrived at Art Stiles' B&B just after one in the afternoon. I parked in the guest lot, grabbed the Browning and silencer I kept when I was on the task force from the glove compartment, checked the magazine, and attached the silencer. I got out and tucked it under my suit jacket.

I opened the picket gate and walked the length of the grounds to the backyard of the house.

Art was on a ladder, giving the green trim on the second floor window shutters a fresh coat.

Monica Stiles sat in the shade at a patio table. She wore reading glasses and was studying what looked like account books.

I walked on the soft grass.

Neither heard my approach until I neared the ladder and Monica looked up at me.

"Art!" Monica called.

Art looked at Monica just as I kicked the ladder out from under him and he fell fifteen feet to the lawn. The ladder and can of green paint landed on top of him.

"Art!" Monica yelled as she ran to him.

I turned and punched Monica in the jaw. Not hard enough to do serious damage, just hard enough to put her down and out for a bit.

Under the ladder, Art moaned.

His hair, shirt, and face were covered in green paint.

I grabbed the ladder, lifted it, and shoved it out of the way.

Art looked at me.

"Jack," Art said.

I grabbed him by the hair and dragged him ten feet, then let him go.

"Get up," I said.

"Jack," Art said.

I pulled the Browning.

"Get up or I'll put two in your brain right now."

Art stood up.

"Tell me how it went down, Art," I said.

"What, Jack?" Art said. "What went down?"

"You and Peterson were on Eddie Crist's payroll as informers," I said.

"Jack, I don't know what . . ."

I stuck the Browning against Art's forehead.

"I saw your names on his list," I said. "I'll count to three, starting with two."

Art looked at me.

"Two," I said.

"I needed the money, Jack," Art blurted out.

I lowered the Browning.

"Monica was sick with cancer," Art said. "The department covered most of it, but not all. The operations, the private doctors, it added up to more than I made in five years. I was desperate for cash."

"Peterson?" I said.

"We were partners," Art said. "He went along with it for me. Once we got in, we couldn't get out. We never figured on the task force, your investigation."

In the background, Monica was on her stomach, crawling toward us.

"You gave Michael Crist the location of my witness?" I said.

Art nodded.

"No choice," Art said.

363

"You had a choice," I said. "You always have a choice."

Art shook his head.

"Once you're in, you're in," he said. "They would have killed us if we didn't deliver. I had Monica to think about. I couldn't take the money and not deliver."

Monica stood up.

"What are you saying, Art?" Monica said.

"He's saying that along with his partner, Dave Peterson, he had my witness killed twelve years ago," I said. "Isn't that right, Art?"

Monica stood in front of Art.

"Along with my wife," I said.

"Is this true, Art?" Monica said.

Art nodded.

"Oh, Art," Monica said. "How could you do such a thing?"

"Thirty-six thousand a year plus benefits," Art said. "Your private care cost fifty thousand a year, how else was I supposed to pay for that? Huh? Moonlight as a security guard? Tell me, Monica, how?"

"Stand aside, Monica," I said.

Monica turned around and looked at the Browning aimed at Art.

"No."

"I said stand aside."

"No."

"Monica, please step aside so we can discuss this," Art said.

"Discuss?" Monica said. "There's blood in his eyes."

I punched Monica a second time, this time putting her down and out.

"At least you didn't kill her," Art said.

"She didn't do anything except get sick," I said.

Art nodded.

"You want to hear about Carol?" he whispered.

"I do."

"This Michael Crist was crazy, Jack," Art said. "He wanted your witness dead, he wanted you dead, the FBI, everybody. We gave him the location. We had no choice. Dave, me, we were taking five grand a week by then. He would have killed us and our families if we didn't. After the witness disappeared, he wanted you and the FBI next. We told him, convinced him that to kill a cop was a death sentence for his old man. He backed off, but insisted you be sent a message. It wasn't supposed to . . . she wasn't . . . it all turned to shit, Jack."

"Who murdered Carol, Art?" I said.

"Michael sent one of his rank and file to your house," Art said. "He was supposed to make sure you backed off the investigation.

We thought you were home."

"We?" I said. "You and Peterson?"

"We checked the duty roster," Art said. "It said you took a few days off. How were we supposed to know it was a fake schedule because you were working for the feds?"

"And?"

"When he came out of your house, he never said a word," Art said. "Not a fucking word about . . ."

"You drove him to my house?" I said.

"Michael insisted."

"Michael insisted, is that what you said?"

"Jack, it's not what you . . ."

"Shut your mouth," I said.

Art was smart enough to shut his mouth.

"You drove him to my house," I said. "What did you do, wait in the car?"

Art nodded.

"And then?"

"We took him back to Michael's apartment in town," Art said. "We thought all he did was throw a scare into you, make a few threats. That kinda shit. It wasn't until later we knew what went down. By then it was too late."

"So you fucked the investigation and you fucked me," I said.

"Jack, it wasn't . . ."

I smacked Art in the face with the Browning. He fell bleeding to the lawn.

"My wife is dead. My daughter has V8 Juice for brains. I spent ten years drunk so I didn't have to face that, so don't tell me it wasn't," I said.

Art wiped blood from his nose and mouth and spit out a chipped tooth.

"The man who killed Carol?" I said.

"After we . . . the news broke, Michael had him killed," Art said. "I think he did it himself."

"Well," I said.

"Yeah," Art said.

I raised the Browning.

"Just tell me what tipped you off," Art said.

"You don't buy a two-million dollar bed and breakfast on a cop's pension," I said. "I suspected, but didn't know for sure until I saw your name on Crist's list."

"Sure," Art said and lowered his head.

I stuck the Browning against Art's head.

"Monica?" Art said.

"She'll get your pension and keep this place," I said. "You have insurance?"

"Some."

"Good."

The Browning was hot in my hand.

I squeezed the trigger, but couldn't pull it.

Seconds ticked by and with each passing one, we both knew I wouldn't kill him.

"Fuck," I said and cracked Art's skull with the Browning.

53

Eddie Crist was resting in bed when I arrived at his mansion. Doctor Richards saw me beforehand in the kitchen. We had tea together with tiny almond cookies.

"Mr. Crist doesn't have much strength left," Richards said. "I'm afraid his end is closer than anticipated. Ten days, two weeks, it's difficult to say."

"But he can see me?" I said.

"You won't upset him?"

"I think he'll be very glad to see me."

"Let's finish our tea and I'll tell him you're here."

I carried tea and cookies on a silver tray to Crist's bedroom. He sat up in bed while I poured cups for both of us and served cookies.

"When I was a little boy, once a week my mother would walk to the local bakery and return home with a box of almond cookies," Crist said. "The box would sit on the counter tied up with that white string all day until dinner time. Sunday dinner was at four and I couldn't wait for my mother to untie that string."

I popped a cookie into my mouth and washed it down with a sip of tea.

Crist bit into a cookie, chewed, and looked at me. His face was a mask of death, but his eyes were alive and alert.

"So, you bring news?" Crist said.

"Yes."

"Tell me."

I told him.

We ate cookies and drank tea.

When I finished, Crist said, "And this detective, there is no doubt he is the man responsible for your wife and not my son?"

"Along with his partner who died several years ago," I said. "Your son gave the order to scare me, not to harm my wife. She surprised him and he panicked. They covered it up to protect their own interests. He tried to make it look like rape and used an object from the bathroom, probably. Michael had him killed afterward or did it himself."

"He was a friend of yours, this detective?"

"Was."

"The man's wife?"

"Innocent of everything. She'll be taken

care of," I said.

Crist nodded.

"Where is this detective now?"

"Trunk of my car."

Crist reached for a remote on the night-stand and pressed a button. Two wingtips immediately entered the bedroom.

"There is a man in the trunk of Mr. Bekker's car," Crist said. "Bring him here to me."

I held out my car keys to a wingtip.

Crist looked at me. "Do you want to wait in my study?"

"I think so," I said.

I walked to the door.

"Bekker?" Crist said.

I paused and turned around.

"I would have beaten you in court even with your witness," Crist said.

"Probably, and I would have kept trying," I said.

Crist nodded.

"See you around," Crist said.

"Yeah," I said and closed the door behind me.

54

Twenty-one days passed in a blink.

I visited Regan daily.

We spent a great deal of time coloring. I got quite good at it. Occasionally, I would catch Regan stealing a glimpse of my work. We ate a lot of peanut butter, jelly, and banana sandwiches. Most days, Janet came with me. A few times, Mark came with us. Turns out, he's pretty handy with a crayon himself.

Father Thomas said Regan made tremendous strides during that time and when I asked if it would be possible for her to leave the grounds with me for a day. He said that he would give it serious consideration.

I spent several hours each day with Mark. We played ball and worked on his cutter and I could see the budding manhood in his young face. He started to put on weight.

Janet visited my trailer every other day.

We found a rhythm.

It was good.

Walt came to visit the trailer several times. We grilled burgers with Oz, drank root beer, and watched ball games. He didn't mention Art Stiles until the third visit.

"A missing persons report was filed on Art Stiles by his wife," Walt said. "Have you heard about that?"

"No," I said.

"Art's wife . . . Monica, you remember her?"

"Yes."

"She claimed he just disappeared," Walt said. "Left and never came back. Don't you find that odd for a man like Art?"

"Things happen," I said.

"They do," Walt said.

He looked at me.

"They do," he said again. "So, listen. That Mickey Mouse PI license you have, feel like putting it to use? I have a case that's going to civil court. A married couple. Nice. They could use some help."

"Leave me their phone number," I said.

"Call me at the office tomorrow," Walt said.

On the morning of the twenty-first day, I watched a sedan enter the beach and drive toward my trailer. I was sipping coffee and smoking a cigarette. The sedan arrived just as I was stubbing the cigarette out in an ashtray.

The wingtip I'd handed my keys to in Crist's bedroom got out from behind the wheel and opened the rear door. He didn't say anything, but nodded to me in recognition.

Crist's personal attorney, Frank Kagan, stepped out, straightened his suit jacket, and walked to me.

I stood up.

We shook hands.

"Would you like some coffee?" I said.

"I would, yes," Kagan said.

I filled a mug for Kagan and he sat in a chair and sipped.

We looked at the beach.

The tide was rolling in, crashing against the rocks.

Gulls were making a racket.

"Mr. Crist passed away at two-forty in the morning," Kagan said. "He went peacefully in his sleep."

I watched the gulls do battle over a dead fish that came in with the tide.

"A few days before he passed, Mr. Crist requested that you attend his funeral," Kagan said.

That largest of the gulls flew away with

his prize.

"I'll be there," I said.

55

Fall comes late around here and isn't much different from late summer. The main difference is the nighttime temperatures drop into the low fifties, and it gets dark earlier. Otherwise, the sun is warm, the surfers take to the waves, and the gulls continue to battle each other for survival.

On one such fall day, I picked up Janet, Mark, and even Molly, and we rode to the hospital to celebrate Regan's eighteenth birthday.

It was a big day.

Mark gave Regan an Etch A Sketch as a gift and showed her how to use it. She took to it immediately. The control of the lines appealed to her sense of order, I suppose. At least it was a step up from crayons.

I asked the question I needed to ask.

Father Thomas answered it by finally giving permission for Regan to travel home with us. Sister Mary Martin came along, of course, but it was a giant stride and a major event in our lives.

Regan toted along coloring books and crayons and her new security blanket, the Etch A Sketch, but didn't touch any of them. Thomas explained to me that the coloring and sketching represented order in Regan's life, that it was something she could guide and control, unlike the events she witnessed as a child.

I understood.

Oz came over with extra beach chairs.

Janet and Mark tossed a Frisbee by the water.

Molly chased gulls twice her size. What would she have done if she caught one?

Regan, Sister Mary Martin, and I took up positions in chairs where we could watch the ocean come in and go out.

Regan didn't speak or show any outward emotion, but she watched and observed everything in her quiet way.

Late in the afternoon, Oz fired up the grill and we gathered round while burgers and dogs sizzled.

Life is one, big ironic surprise, Crist had told me and he was right.

We had a birthday cake with whipped cream frosting.

As we watched the sun cross the sky and

begin to lower, Molly jumped on Regan's lap and rubbed her ears on my daughter's stomach.

I looked at Janet.

The fingers on her right hand were covering her mouth. She was fighting back tears.

Regan didn't speak.

But after a few moments, she moved her hand to stroke Molly's back.

I tried very hard to maintain composure as Sister Mary Martin lost hers.

Molly began to purr.

It wasn't much.

Just everything.

ABOUT THE AUTHOR

Al Lamanda is the author of four mystery novels. His works include *Dunston Falls, Walking Homeless, Running Homeless,* and *Sunset.* A native New Yorker, he presently resides in Maine.

CPSIA information can be obtained
at www.ICGtesting.com
Printed in the USA
FFOW031406220113
740FF